A PARROT TO DIE FOR

A MARIPOSA BEACH COZY MYSTERY
BOOK 7

K.C. AMES

17th Street BOOKS

STAY CONNECTED

Visit my website to connect with me on social media and for more information about my books:

www.KCAmes.com

Get a free ebook featuring the recipes of the delicious dishes featured in this book when you join my mailing list. Plus, get updates on new releases, deals, recommend reads, and more by visiting:

www.KCAmes.com/Recipes

CHAPTER ONE

THE JANUARY SUN WAS SCORCHING ON LAPA MOUNTAIN'S
dirt trails. Dana Kirkpatrick drove on those trails in her mint
condition cherry red 1947 Jeep Willys she nicknamed Big Red.

The sun reflected off its shiny hood. Dana's sun-bleached
hair was swept back by the wind, and her laughter filled the air
as the jeep snaked up the mountain. Beside her, Courtney Lowe
— her best friend from San Francisco — was white-knuckling
the heavy-duty grab handle with her right hand as the fingers of
her left hand dug into the dashboard. Her eyes were wide with a
mix of amazement and trepidation over the wild ride in the
jeep.

"Just make sure you don't drive off the side of this cliff,"
Courtney remarked, casting an incredulous glance at Dana,
who grinned cheekily in response.

Lapa Mountain was named after the Spanish word for the
vibrant macaw parrots that were frequently spotted around
these parts. They were way off the beaten path about thirty
miles from Mariposa Beach. A lush forest surrounded them, and
the blue waters of Mariposa Beach were visible in the distance.

The remoteness and poor roads up there had probably

allowed the area to remain pristine since it was protected from the destructive nature of humans.

Big Red was built for this terrain. With every twist and turn, the road grew rougher, as the views were more rewarding. On one side of the mountain path, the dense foliage was so lush it seemed to close in on them. The view from the edge of the cliff was breathtaking, with rivers and valleys converging towards the sparkling coastline.

Courtney was nervous during the ride because of the sharp turns on a rocky road, which Dana handled by barely easing off the gas pedal.

"Dana," Courtney began, trying to keep her voice even, "could you maybe, I don't know, ease up a bit?"

Dana threw her a sidelong glance. "Court, we're in a legendary jeep here. It stormed across Europe during World War II. She's made for this kind of stuff."

"Well, we're not storming the beaches of Normandy, so slow down, General Patton," Courtney said with a smirk. "Besides, if we go tumbling down the mountainside, this legendary jeep won't save us."

Dana chuckled. "I promise, I've done this a thousand times. Trust me, all right?" And with that, she hit the gas pedal even harder, sending them soaring over a bumpy stretch. Courtney yelped, gripping the dashboard for dear life.

As the jeep's tires clung to the mountain's curves, Dana felt more alive than ever. This was her paradise, far away from the hustle and bustle of San Francisco which she had left for Mariposa Beach. The sense of freedom, the raw connection with nature. It was everything she had yearned for when she ditched the big city living sitting in bumper-to-bumper traffic and foul-smelling air.

To Dana, the Big Red wasn't just a vehicle; it was a symbol

of her new life and adventures in Mariposa Beach; her passport to a wild and open tropical paradise.

Just then, as if on cue, a colorful macaw swooped down in front of them, its radiant feathers catching the sunlight as it landed on a nearby branch, checking them out. Courtney gasped, momentarily forgetting her nerves.

"Look at that!" she exclaimed. "It's stunning!"

The beauty of the bird finally got Dana to slow down as they both took a moment to admire the beautiful parrot.

"That's the lapa. A scarlet macaw. Isn't it beautiful? Makes the ride worth it, doesn't it?" Dana said, entranced with the parrot.

Courtney smiled. "For views like this, maybe I can endure a little more of your mountain road hotdogging. Just... promise me we'll get down in one piece?"

Dana laughed, reaching over to pat Courtney's knee reassuringly. "Promise. Now, buckle up, we're heading to my favorite spot."

"Oh, don't worry. I'm not letting go of this bar until you put this beast in park." They both laughed as Dana got Big Red back on the move up the mountain and deeper into the forest, excited to see what else Lapa Mountain had in store for them.

It was January, which is one of the warmest months in Mariposa Beach with scorching sun and balmy nights, unlike in the winter wonderlands up north. Costa Rica had two seasons. Wet and dry. The dry season ran from December to April, which was the peak of the busy tourist season.

But you wouldn't find too many tourists all the way up there. The green canopy also offered a respite from the heat down on the beach. Not that it was cold. The mountain's height and ocean breezes made it cooler and more refreshing than the lower areas.

You could smell the ocean's salt in the forest's aroma. The combination was invigorating, a tonic for the senses.

The dichotomy between the sweltering beach town and the breezy mountain was one of the area's unique charms. On the beach, people sunbathed and surfed, while hikers in the mountains enjoyed the cool shade of the forest and the sound of streams.

A quick drive in Costa Rica can take you from hot beaches to cool mountains. For the people of Mariposa Beach, it was a luxury they never took for granted. They knew that while others were shoveling snow or huddling for warmth; they had the best of both worlds — the sun-kissed beaches and the refreshing breezes of Lapa Mountain.

Dana drove Big Red into the clearing, letting out a sigh of contentment as she killed the engine. "That was fun," she said. Courtney looked at her askance, not seeming to agree.

The landscape stretched before them, a surprising expanse of grassy meadow nestled within the dense forest, akin to a mini savannah. The sun cast golden hues upon the tall grass, making it dance in the gentle breeze.

Courtney glanced around, her eyes widening in awe as she forgot the rough ride to get there. "Wow," she murmured, "this is... incredible."

Dana nodded, her own eyes sparkling with pride. "This is one of my favorite spots. It feels like the heart of the mountain."

"You come out here often?"

"No. This is my third time."

Before either could further comment on the beauty of the clearing, a shadow passed overhead. Then another, and another. They looked up to find themselves surrounded by a kaleidoscope of red as dozens of scarlet macaws swirled in the skies above them. The vibrant birds flew close, their wingtips almost grazing over their heads.

Their raucous calls filled the air, a chorus of wild melodies that echoed the spirit of freedom and untamed beauty. They rendered both Dana and Courtney speechless, their eyes tracking the mesmerizing dance of the macaws.

"I've never seen so many," Dana said in awe.

"It's like... a dream," Courtney whispered, her voice tinged with wonder. The tableau was nothing short of cinematic, a once-in-a-lifetime spectacle.

But in the blink of an eye, the dreamlike atmosphere shattered.

A rustling in the underbrush caught Dana's attention, and she turned to see a towering figure emerging from the forest's edge. The man, rugged and wearing an unruly beard reminiscent of Grizzly Adams, had a wild look in his eyes. Sunlight glinted menacingly off the large machete he wielded, and every step he took toward them was filled with purpose and aggression.

Courtney gasped, her earlier amazement replaced by a palpable fear. "Dana..." she whispered urgently.

Dana, her instincts kicking in, reached for the ignition. But the jeep refused to start, the engine emitting a desperate sputter before falling silent. Dana felt panicked. The macaws, sensing the tension, scattered with raucous cries, leaving the clearing in an eerie quiet.

The man was closing the distance fast, his eyes locked on the two women.

"Out of the jeep!" he bellowed, his voice echoing ominously through the clearing.

Dana's mind raced. Run? Confront him? Every option seemed fraught with danger.

The gruff stranger raised his machete, his intent clear, "I won't ask again."

CHAPTER TWO

Dana's heart was pounding, and Courtney gripped her arm as they got out of the jeep and saw the mountain man with a machete.

As the man approached, his intense gaze flitted between them, to the jeep, and back to the women. His face twisted in confusion, and then realization. "You're not poachers," he said, his tone filled with a mix of surprise and relief.

Courtney, still visibly shaken, didn't reply. But Dana, ever the voice of reason, stepped forward slightly, her voice defiant yet calm. "What? No. We're just enjoying nature up here."

The grizzled man's posture relaxed, and with a swift motion he slid the machete back into its sheath. "Sorry for scaring you gals. I thought you were poachers. Been seeing more than usual the last few days."

Dana, her initial fear replaced by anger and annoyance, folded her arms. "You could've just asked instead of charging at us with a weapon like a madman. You almost gave me a heart attack."

"I have to come out aggressively to scare them off. Some of these poachers are dangerous, so I need to get the upper hand."

Dana was still upset and wanted to read him the riot act, but her curiosity got the better of her. "So, um, what are they poaching for all the way up here?"

His gaze shifted upward, following the bright flashes of red amidst the trees. "You saw what they're after. The parrots." His voice held a hint of sadness, but there was an underlying steely determination to keep the parrots safe.

The birds seemed to sense the tension was over and returned, as if gawking at the weird humans below. The cacophony from the macaws seemed even louder now, their vibrant colors painting the trees with life. "My name is Agostino Espada. I look after the parrots," he said, his chest puffing out slightly with pride.

Courtney, finding her voice again, chimed in, "But why would anyone want to harm these beautiful creatures?"

His expression grew darker. "They don't just want to harm them; they want to sell them. These magnificent birds are captured and handed off to middlemen. Then, eventually, they're sold for a lot of money. Capturing and selling macaws is illegal in Costa Rica, but the money in the illicit trade... it's too tempting for some."

Dana frowned, empathy clear in her eyes. "That's terrible, Agostino."

A small smile played on his lips. "Everyone calls me Tino."

Dana's anger toward Tino was gone. He was just protecting the majestic birds.

Courtney looked back at the jeep.

"Dana, why wouldn't Big Red start?" she asked, breaking Dana's reverie on the parrots.

Dana walked back to the jeep and climbed inside. She patted the dashboard affectionately. "Well, Big Red has seen seven decades. Occasionally, she needs a moment." She gave a wry grin. Turning the ignition key again, she winced as the motor labored in vain.

Courtney threw her hands up. "Fantastic. Big Red's down and we're stranded on this mountain." She looked at her phone. "Without signal."

"Just needs a jump," Tino chimed in, his tone helpful.

Courtney smirked, crossing her arms. "Sure. I'll just dial Triple A. They'll definitely race right up this mountain."

Tino scratched his beard thoughtfully. "I have jumper cables back at my place," he offered.

The two women exchanged glances, realizing the isolation of their location.

"How far is it from here?" Dana asked.

"It's a short walk. About two miles. Once there, I can drive you both back with my truck and get your jeep back up and running," Tino proposed.

Dana hesitated. It was an unexpected gesture from a man who, until a short while ago, had been charging at them with a long blade. But that was just a misunderstanding, Dana thought. Besides, they were short on alternatives.

"Thank you, Tino," Dana said. Courtney's eyes darted between Dana and the dense forest, her skepticism clear. She looked at her phone again, hoping for a miracle. Nothing. No bars.

"No towers in this neck of the woods," Tino remarked, a chuckle in his voice.

Courtney sighed in resignation.

Dana leaned closer to Courtney, whispering, "The sun will set soon, Court. We need to move."

Courtney nodded, albeit grudgingly. "All right, Tino," Dana said decisively. "Lead the way."

THE PATH to Tino's place turned out to be far more challenging than Dana had imagined. Each step felt treacherous, with loose gravel and underbrush threatening to trip them up and pull them down the steep cliff. It was a steady incline that made her muscles ache, and she could hear Courtney's strained breathing behind her.

The path became so narrow that they had to fall into a single file to walk through it.

"Why didn't you mention the hike was like something out of an adventure film?" Dana snapped at Tino as they navigated an even narrower section of the trail.

Tino chuckled, amused. "You two are half my age! Figured you could handle a little walk in the woods."

As they curved around a cliff, the Pacific Ocean stretched out in front of them. She could see the shimmering gold from the sun where it hit the water. The view was breathtaking, but the sheer drop just a footstep away made the palms of her hand clammy. Every time Dana looked down, her stomach flipped.

Courtney held on to the back of Dana's shirt as she had clutched the jeep's grab handle, her knuckles white. "Why the heck does he live here?" she murmured under her breath, her gaze fixed on the narrow path.

Tino seemed unfazed, strolling ahead with the confidence of someone who had walked this route countless times. It was as though the life-threatening drop beside him was no more significant than a puddle after a light rain.

After what felt like hours, Tino stopped and pointed ahead. "We're here," he said. There, perched dramatically on the cliff's edge, was a house. It was rustic, with wooden walls and a thatched roof, almost camouflaged against the backdrop of the dense woods.

"That's my home," Tino announced, a hint of pride in his voice.

The house's remoteness set off alarm bells for Dana and Courtney. They exchanged a wary look, realizing it wasn't just away from the hustle and bustle of the world. It was literally in the middle of nowhere. Every worst-case scenario played out in Dana's mind. Why had they agreed to this? He could chop them up with that machete and no one would ever find them up here.

Courtney leaned closer to Dana, her voice barely audible. "Dana, what if he's... you know, not just a bird protector? We're directly delivering ourselves to a possible psycho on a silver platter."

Dana tried to stay calm, her mind racing. "Stay alert," she whispered back. "Let's just get Big Red up and running. Then we can get out of here."

They approached the house cautiously, aware of how vulnerable they were. Every creak and rustle of the trees in the wind heightened their sense of danger.

Tino, seemingly oblivious to their concerns, led the way. "Let's get those cables and get you two back on the road."

Following the stranger through the woods to his place made Dana feel anxious. Had she made a mistake?

CHAPTER THREE

The closer Dana and Courtney got to Tino's home, the more it resembled an idyllic homestead rather than the lair of some twisted serial killer. The scent of damp earth and a vegetable garden wafted on the breeze.

Tino's views into the open waters of the Pacific were amazing from up there. She jokingly expected to be able to see Australia.

Dana was impressed with the garden, which burst with the colors of vegetables. Tomatoes gleamed like rubies, bell peppers in bright reds, yellows and greens, and beds of leafy greens like lettuce and spinach. Dana recognized many of the plants from her own garden back at Mariposa Beach. There were also neat rows of herbs and flowering plants that attracted bees and butterflies.

Beyond the garden, a bed of purple and white orchids thrived. Past that, trees heavy with ripe mangos and avocados swayed gently in the breeze, their leaves rustling softly. Banana and plantain trees stood tall, their fruits hanging like golden lanterns.

Feathered chickens roamed free and played with goats. The soft clucks and bleats created a symphony of farm life.

Suddenly, a cheerful bark sounded, and a border collie with a glossy coat and bright eyes darted towards them. The dog circled them once and then, with tail wagging furiously, came to a halt in front of Dana, offering its head for a pat.

"That's Ringo," Tino said with a smile. "He's quite the charmer."

Dana kneeled and ruffled Ringo's fur, delight clear in her eyes. The dog's exuberant energy was infectious, and his presence melted away some of the lingering tension from being in the remote home of a stranger.

"It's hard to be scared of a place with a dog like Ringo around," Dana whispered to Courtney.

Courtney, who had been watching the chickens with amusement, turned to Dana. "I have to admit, it's not exactly the creepy mountain lair I was imagining."

Dana smirked. "And I was trying not to think of Buffalo Bill's little dog Precious from *Silence of the Lambs*."

Courtney gave her a *don't you dare go there* look as Dana laughed.

Tino, fetching a basket of fresh vegetables, overheard her. He chuckled. "If I had a dollar for every time someone thought I was like the Unabomber because of my remote home and my beard, I'd probably be able to buy a new truck."

His candidness further eased the tension, and the three shared a laugh. The farm was beautiful and showed a man living peacefully with nature, which was different from what they'd expected.

As Dana and Courtney continued to take in the surroundings of Tino's homestead, a structure off to the side caught Dana's eye. Beyond the garden and the orchard, set against the backdrop of dense rainforest, stood a large, graceful aviary.

The aviary was a masterwork of design and functionality. Tall and spacious, it was made of a blend of bamboo and steel, creating a sturdy yet organic feel. The top was a finely meshed netting, allowing sunlight to filter through and draped shadows to play on the ground. Colorful vines and tropical flowers grew with the bamboo. Wild butterflies fluttered about.

Inside, the birds had ample space to fly. The birds had different wooden perches and a small waterfall leading to a pond.

There were bananas, mangoes, and papaya on sticks and in bowls for the parrots to munch on. And there were also many tropical plants and flowers that looked like their natural environment. Dana saw brilliantly colored parrots, finches, and even a toucan or two, all moving with an ease that suggested they felt safe and protected.

Courtney, drawn to the vibrant spectacle, asked, "What's with all these birds, Tino?"

Tino's face softened, pride and a touch of sorrow clear in his eyes. "This is my bird sanctuary. Over the years, I've found injured birds, or rescued ones trapped by poachers, or rescues that had been kept in horrid conditions in pet shops. Some can't be returned to the wild because of their injuries or because they've been too domesticated."

He paused, his gaze sweeping over the aviary, clearly cherishing every bird there. "So, I built this place for them. A haven where they can live as close to a natural life as possible. If I can't release them back into the wild, they can stay with me, safe."

Tino's dedication moved Dana. "It's beautiful," she said. "Not just the aviary itself, but the thought and love you've poured into it."

Tino shrugged modestly. "Nature's been kind to me. It's the least I can do to give back."

Dana nodded, her earlier apprehensions about Tino long

gone. "It's not just a sanctuary for the birds, is it? It's a sanctuary for you, too."

Tino looked at the two women, a genuine smile gracing his rugged features. "You're right. This place, these birds... they've saved me just as much as I've saved them. It's why I get so protective of them."

As they made their way back to the house, Tino gestured towards a small veranda with a couple of hand-carved wooden chairs. "Can I offer you ladies something to drink? Maybe some cas juice? It's pretty refreshing."

Courtney glanced at Dana, who shook her head gently. "Thank you, Tino, but we really should get going before darkness settles in. These mountains can get quite tricky to navigate in the dark," Dana said.

"Of course, I understand," Tino replied, leading them towards a rustic wooden shed next to the carport. He opened its creaky door and rummaged around for a moment before emerging with a pair of heavy-duty jumper cables, holding them up for the women to see.

Dana smiled, relieved. "Perfect. We'll be back on our way in no time."

It was then that Dana's eyes fell on Tino's truck. It was an old yet sturdy-looking vehicle, built for the rough terrains of the mountains, but it was unmistakably a two-seater.

Courtney glanced at Dana, raising an eyebrow. "Um, Dana? There might be a slight logistical issue here."

"I guess one of us is riding shotgun and one of us will be in the back of the truck."

Tino, sensing their hesitation, chimed in. "The bed's got a thick padding, and it's not far. You'll be fine."

"Shotgun!" Courtney shouted with a smirk.

Dana smiled, understanding the rules of calling shotgun since childhood. "Well played," she said.

They all chuckled. As Tino prepared the truck and Dana settled into the back, Ringo jumped in to join her, much to her delight. She had to admit that despite the unexpected adventure, the day had turned out to be quite an experience.

The pickup's engine rumbled to life, its sound echoing faintly against the surrounding mountains. Tino drove the truck on the same narrow path they had used before. Dana felt nervous, and her palms became sweaty.

Courtney looked back through the window of the pickup with disbelief. "You've got to be kidding me," she mouthed, as she gripped the sides of the truck tightly.

"Isn't there another route? Like a main road, perhaps?" Dana asked through the small open window between the bed of the pickup and the cab, her voice edged with desperation.

Tino glanced her way, his eyes steady. "There is, but it circles around a big portion of the mountain. Going that way, it's a much longer drive. We'd be driving in the dark for sure. This way it's ten minutes."

"But this path..." Dana began, staring down at the terrifying drop just a few feet from her. The thought of the vehicle skidding off the path and down the mountain sent shivers down her spine. Or driving over a big boulder that would catapult her out of the back of the truck down the side of the cliff like a cannonball. She didn't even have a seat belt to keep her in the truck.

"No worries," Tino said gently. I've driven this path countless times. I can drive it with my eyes closed."

"Oh, no, please don't do that, Eyes open, front and center," Dana said. Tino laughed.

Dana's mind raced. She felt the reassuring warmth of Ringo next to her, the dog's calm demeanor a stark contrast to her own heightened state of anxiety.

She took deep breaths and focused on Ringo and not the scary, enormous cliff.

Tino continued to maneuver the truck down the winding path. Every jolt, every minor skid of the tires on loose gravel made Dana's heart leap into her throat. She kept her eyes fixed ahead, not daring to glance towards the edge, but the sheer drop was always there, a peripheral menace.

The Pacific Ocean in the distance was now bathed in the orange and pink hues of the setting sun, a beautiful yet cruel irony given the treacherous journey.

And then, just as Dana felt they might be past the worst of it, the truck's rear wheel hit a patch of dried debris. The vehicle lurched sideways, skidding precariously close to the edge. Dana's heart stopped. Every muscle tensed, her fingers digging into the seat, eyes squeezed shut, and her other arm wrapped tightly around Ringo.

For a split second, time seemed to freeze, the world narrowing down to the roar of the engine and the distant crashing waves below.

Then, just as suddenly, the truck jolted back onto the path, regaining its traction. Tino quickly brought it to a stop, his normally calm face pale and taut.

For a moment, no one spoke; the only sound was the heavy breathing of the passengers and the ticking of the cooling engine.

Dana slowly opened her eyes, relieved they hadn't tumbled over the side of the cliff. "That was too close," she whispered.

From the front, Courtney let out a shaky laugh. "I won't complain about Big Red anymore."

CHAPTER FOUR

PARROTS FILLED THE CLEARING WHERE BIG RED HAD stalled, flying, and making loud calls that echoed through the trees.

Dana and Courtney stepped out of the truck, the scary drive over here forgotten as they looked around in wonder. There were parrots all around them — on trees, on the ground, and in the sky. The sight was nothing short of magical.

Courtney began snapping photos, the joy evident in her eyes. "This is absolutely amazing, Dana," she whispered, afraid to disrupt the natural symphony around them.

Her friend nodded, her gaze fixed on a playful pair that danced in the air before settling on Big Red's hood. "It's like a secret paradise," she murmured.

Tino, leaning against his truck, watched the two women with a hint of a smile. "This is why I do what I do," he said softly. "This place... it's become a sanctuary for them. I've watched over it for years."

Dana turned to him, her previous apprehensions now replaced with genuine curiosity. "I can see why you want to protect these magnificent creatures."

"Word got around the district that some poachers had gotten wind of this place," he said, his eyes distant. "They know the parrots flock here, and the price they can get for even one of these magnificent creatures... it's a temptation too big for some. That's why I've been on edge lately."

"I'm sorry we misunderstood earlier. And thank you for everything you're doing for these birds." Dana approached him, extending a hand.

Tino took her hand, giving it a firm shake. "I should be the one apologizing. I let my fears get the best of me, greeting you with my machete. But I can't let anything happen to these birds. They're like family to me."

Courtney, having finished her impromptu photo session, joined them. "It's incredible what you're doing, Tino. Protecting them, taking care of the injured ones. You're like their guardian angel."

"Never thought of it that way. I just can't stand by and let these birds be taken."

They turned their attention to Big Red. Tino began hooking up the cables and firing up his truck, breathing life to Big Red. After a couple of minutes, he shouted at Dana over the revved-up engine. "Try it now."

On the first attempt, Big Red sputtered, coughed, and then came back to life. Dana and Courtney exchanged happy glances.

"Thank you, Tino!"

As the sun began its descent, they stood together a while longer, watching the parrots. The free birds were a beautiful reminder of nature's balance and the contrast between those who profited from it and those who protected it like Tino. He wanted them to be free birds, the profiteers wanted to put them in cages. Clip their wings so they couldn't escape.

The tranquility they were enjoying was disrupted by the distant sound of a motorboat.

Dana's heart raced as Tino tensed up. He ran to the passenger side of his truck, and from the glove compartment he grabbed a pair of binoculars. He aimed the binoculars toward the ocean and peered through them, his face hardening with determination.

The boat was off in the distance, heading toward the coast. "Fishing boat?" she asked, squinting. Deep-sea fishing was popular with the tourists.

Tino shook his head, still looking through the binoculars. "Not on this side of the bay and heading in this direction instead of towards Mariposa Beach. And that's a power boat, not the catamarans that take tourists out fishing." Without looking away from the approaching boat, he added, "Dana, you and Courtney need to get out of here. Now." His voice held an urgency that left no room for debate.

"What are you going to do?" Dana asked.

"Protect my birds. You girls, go!" Tino said, more forcibly than before.

Courtney clutched Dana's arm, her eyes wide. "Dana, let's get out here, please."

"But what about him? We can't just leave him!" Dana protested.

"This is his turf. We can't help him if we're out here without even a phone signal. Let's at least get to where we can call for help. That's the best we can do."

"You're right," Dana replied, even as concern for the man gnawed at her. She watched as Tino quickly jumped into his pickup truck, Ringo eagerly hopping in beside him.

Before they could say another word, Tino's pickup roared to life, dust and gravel flying as he raced down the narrow path.

The speed at which he maneuvered the truck was astonishing, and Dana held her breath, praying he would be safe.

"Dana, we need to go!" Courtney said.

As they drove away, the distant roar of the speedboat grew fainter, but the worry about Tino remained. They would do everything in their power to ensure that the sanctuary stayed untouched and the brave guardian of the macaws safe.

THEY WERE BACK on the main road, the dense canopy giving way to the open sky. The stresses of their adventure were slowly fading, replaced by the familiar sights and sounds of life around Mariposa Beach. Street vendors sold fresh fruits, children played soccer in the fields, and the shimmering Pacific stretched as far as the eye could see.

Courtney looked relieved. "I'm glad that's over."

Dana, however, still felt a knot in her stomach. Her phone buzzed, signaling the return of a cell signal. Without hesitation, she dialed the number for the closest police substation, which was about twenty miles away. A familiar voice answered.

"This is Officer Freddy Sanchez. How can I help?"

Dana quickly explained the situation, her voice quivering with urgency. The officer's reaction was not what she expected.

"Ah, Tino." Officer Freddy chuckled. "He's been calling us about poachers for years. Most of the time, it's just birdwatchers or tourists like you."

"But there was a speedboat," Dana protested. "And Tino was convinced it was trouble."

Officer Freddy sighed. "Doña Dana, Tino, has a vivid imagination. He's accused local fishermen, kids on jet skis, even researchers of being poachers. Trust me, he can handle himself. Thanks for the concern."

She was flabbergasted. "You're not going to do anything?"

"There's nothing to do," Officer Freddy replied calmly. "If Tino calls us for help, we'll check it out."

Dana hung up. "They brushed me off."

Courtney sighed, rubbing her temples. "It's a small town, Dana. Everyone knows everyone. Maybe they have a point. Tino accused us of being poachers, too."

She had a point. But it didn't feel right, leaving him on his own.

Her grip on the steering wheel tightened. "Tino risked his life for those birds. I can't just sit by and do nothing."

"What's the plan, then?"

"We go back to Mariposa, regroup, and figure out how to help," Dana said with determination.

And with that, the two women continued their journey, the setting sun casting a golden hue on Mariposa Beach. But beneath the beauty, a storm of uncertainty brewed.

CHAPTER FIVE

THE FAMILIAR SOOTHING HUM OF OCEAN WAVES GREETED Dana and Courtney as they stepped into Dana's home. Casa Verde, an expansive villa surrounded by thick tropical greenery and boasting a pristine view of the sea, had become Dana's refuge. It was a stark contrast to her urban Craftsman-style home back in the Cole Valley neighborhood of San Francisco, and it was there, in a remote corner of Costa Rica, that she'd rediscovered herself after the whirlwind of her divorce.

She walked through the dark living room, touching framed photos on the mantel. They were memories of trips, family events, and a recent one of her and Benny smiling in front of a Mariposa Beach sunset.

She picked up her phone and dialed Benny Campos's number. The line trilled once, then twice, before a deep voice answered.

"Hey babe, how's it going?"

"Just got back from Lapa Mountain. Say, do you know Tino Espada?" Benny had grown up in the suburbs of San José, but his family had owned a beach house on Mariposa Beach since before he was born. He had spent a lot of time down there and knew many locals.

"The bird guy from up in the mountains?" Benny asked.

Dana recounted the day's events, her voice becoming more urgent with each word. When she finished, there was silence on the other end.

"What were you doing up there?"

"Enjoying the birds, the scenery... I didn't expect any of this. Benny, the police brushed it off when I called. I'm worried about Tino."

Benny sighed. "You have a big heart. But Tino is a big boy. He knows how to take care of himself. Has been living up there alone for decades."

"Explains why he's so..."

"Odd?" Benny finished Dana's sentence with a chuckle.

"No, eccentric; that's the word I was looking for."

Having grown up in San Francisco, Dana was used to a heavy dose of eccentricity from people, and it was no different in most places she's visited. *How dull and boring would life be if everyone were one hundred percent the same?* Dana thought.

"Just let him be. These boaters were probably just tourists. He sees poachers around every nook and cranny," Benny said.

She frowned. "That doesn't mean we can't do something. Tino may be eccentric, but he doesn't deserve to be ignored."

A pause. Then Benny replied, "All right. Let me make a few calls, see if I can find out more about the boat, maybe push the police a bit."

She felt a rush of relief. "Thank you. I knew I could count on you."

As they hung up, Dana felt a warm glow, a reminder of the unexpected love she'd found in this beautiful coastal town. Despite the chaos, she knew she'd made the right choice coming to Mariposa Beach. Benny was her anchor there, and together they'd face whatever challenges came their way.

"What's the dreamboat's take on this?" Courtney said with a grin, snapping Dana out of her thoughts.

She loved to tease Dana, who had sworn off a new relationship before moving down there to find another one a few months later. Dana gave her an eyeroll, then told her what Benny had said.

"Good, so let the proper authorities take care of things. I'm going to shower. I'm starving," Courtney said, heading upstairs.

Dana checked the time. *Crud.* She had completely lost track of it while being preoccupied with Tino. The two women were meeting Benny for dinner at a restaurant in town in an hour. Dana caught a glimpse of herself in the hallway mirror; she looked like a wind-swept madwoman. And she caught a whiff of her body odor after a day out in the tropics and winced.

She dashed upstairs with Wally, her cat, in tow to hit the shower and get ready for dinner with Benny.

DANA HAD MET Benny when she inherited Casa Verde from her Uncle Blake. Benny had worked as his attorney in Costa Rica for years. She wasn't that close to her estranged uncle, so she was as shocked as anyone when she inherited his Costa Rican property.

As weeks turned into months, Dana found herself spending a lot of time with Benny, discussing property rights, tax implications and, more critically, the lawsuit started by her uncle's estranged son. Benny was relentless in his defense, showcasing a sharp legal acumen that Dana deeply respected. They became closer through intense court sessions and late-night discussions. At first she'd fought her feelings, but after a few months she gave into her heart, and they transitioned from client-lawyer to something more profound.

Mariposa Beach — Que Vista Restaurant

The sound of waves crashing added to the peaceful atmosphere of the Que Vista Restaurant, a popular dining spot in Mariposa Beach.

The restaurant laid out tables right on the golden sand, providing patrons with an intimate dining experience accompanied by the ocean's whispers. The flickering light from tiki torches provided a soft, romantic glow, their bamboo shafts dug firmly into the sand.

Where else could you enjoy a delicious gourmet meal with your bare toes wiggling in the sand?

Dana, Courtney, and Benny sat at a cozy corner table taking in the view of the ocean. The stars shimmered above, adding to the picturesque setting. They chatted animatedly, their laughter echoing the light-hearted atmosphere of the evening.

Maria Rivera, the restaurant's vivacious owner, walked over, her wide smile as warm as the Costa Rican sun. "¡Hola! So good to see you," she greeted, giving Dana and Benny a brief, affectionate hug. "Courtney, you're back for a visit! How nice to see you again."

"I'm impressed with your memory. It's been a few months since I was here, and you remembered my name."

As the evening progressed, their table became a culinary canvas showcasing the rich gastronomy of Costa Rica. The star of the meal was the freshly caught fish, deep-fried to perfection into a mouth-watering and flakey golden crust, its juicy white meat melting in their mouths. Fried yucca was served on the side, its crispy exterior and tender insides complementing the fish beautifully. No Costa Rican meal was complete without the classic combination of fluffy white rice and black beans, also cooked to perfection and delicately flavored with sea salt, red bell peppers, onion, and cilantro. A bowl of lettuce and hearts of palm smothered with a tangy mango vinaigrette completed the feast.

During their enjoyable dinner, the boisterous laughter of a nearby table grabbed Dana's attention. She noticed a large group, evidently not locals, chatting away and clinking their bottles of Pilsen beer in high spirits. While she brushed off their loudness, their topic of conversation piqued Dana's interest.

"...you wouldn't believe the range of exotic birds up there. And you know what they fetch in the international markets? An absolute fortune," a man remarked, causing a ripple of intrigued murmurs amongst the group.

Suspicion replaced the relaxed atmosphere Dana had felt a moment ago. The recent encounter with Tino flashed before her eyes. Could these have been the people in that boat?

CHAPTER SIX

It irritated Dana that neither Benny nor Courtney shared her concern about the group's bird discussion.

"Bird enthusiasts flock to Mariposa Beach all the time. Bird-watching is in the top five activities for tourists coming down here. So I'm not surprised they were talking about birds," Benny said.

"But they weren't just talking about birdwatching. They mentioned the lucrative prices those birds could command on the market," Dana countered.

"It's just casual dinner chatter. Especially after a few beers. Doesn't mean they're involved in illegal activities."

Courtney chimed in, "You're beginning to sound a lot like Tino. Spotting poachers at every corner."

Dana exhaled, letting her shoulders droop. It was clear they didn't view that group with the same level of suspicion as she did.

Maria Rivera again approached their table with a warm smile, interrupting Dana's thoughts. "I hope everything's to your satisfaction," she said, sweeping her hand over their table of now mostly empty dishes.

Benny nodded appreciatively. "Your food never disappoints, Maria."

"And that fresh catch today was especially good. The seas have been generous," Maria said, looking out to the open water.

Dana took a sip of her drink, her eyes scanning the restaurant. "Seems like a busy night. Is there some event we don't know about?"

"I don't think so. It's just the usual influx of tourists at this time of the year. Our busiest," she said excitedly.

"Do you get a lot of birdwatchers?" Dana asked.

"Oh, sure, that's a popular activity here. Not as big as lying on the beach, fishing, and surfing, but it's up there," Maria said.

Benny gave Dana his *told you so* look.

Dana seized the opportunity. "Speaking of birdwatching, have you noticed anything unusual lately? Or anyone talking about more than just... watching birds?"

Maria looked thoughtful. "Not particularly. But then again, I pay little attention to every conversation in the restaurant. Why?"

"It's nothing. Just something I overheard," Dana replied evasively.

Maria nodded, her gaze drifting over to the noisy group. "Some people just get louder after a few drinks." She winked and moved on to the next table.

Dana avoided Benny and Courtney's steely glance. It was pitch dark now and the only light coming in now was from the tiki torches, casting flickering shadows on the sand. The sound of waves crashing added to the ambiance, but Dana's unease remained.

THE NEXT MORNING, Dana took Courtney to her bookstore.

As they entered *Books, Bagels, and Coffee,* they were greeted by just that: the smell of old books and freshly brewed coffee. The coffee and bagel side of the store was owned by her friends Mindy and Leo Salas, a married couple who ran the most popular coffee shop in a fifty-mile radius.

That part of the business was always bustling. The book side, not so much. But Dana found a soothing calmness in looking at the wooden shelves, laden with book titles both new and used, as soft jazz played in the background. She always found the atmosphere of a bookstore inviting and remained excited about owning one, despite the slow pace of the book retail business. *Only stubborn old me opens a bookstore in the digital age*, Dana would say.

Amalfi, a petite young woman with a mop of curly brown hair and glasses perched on her nose, was behind the counter, meticulously arranging a stack of books. She looked up and waved cheerfully as Dana and Courtney entered.

"Morning, Doña Dana. Morning, Courtney," she said, her eyes bright. She was Dana's only employee.

"Morning, Amalfi," Dana replied. "How was yesterday?"

Amalfi's face lit up. "You wouldn't believe it! A group came in, loud and all over the place. They cleared out every travel guidebook on birdwatching we had. And they bought all the maps of the district. It was like they were on some sort of mission, which was good for us. A big sales day!"

"How many were there?" Dana asked.

Amalfi thought about it. "I think there were six of them," she finally replied.

"That's the same number from the restaurant last night," Dana whispered to Courtney.

"If they are birdwatchers, it makes sense they came here to the only bookstore in town to buy books and maps about bird-watching," Courtney said with a grin.

"Do you remember anything else about them?" Dana asked Amalfi.

"They seemed to be in a rush. One of them, tall, bald, with a tattoo of a bird on his neck, kept pushing the others to move faster. And there was talk of a meetup, but I didn't catch the details. He had a strange accent."

American and Canadian tourists were the most common visitors to Mariposa Beach. Amalfi knew their accents well. "Strange, how? Like not an American accent?" Dana prodded.

"No. European. But not like the British or French. Russian, maybe. I'm not sure."

Dana's unease from the previous night returned, this time stronger. "Thanks, Amalfi. Keep an eye out and let me know if they return, okay?"

"Of course, Doña Dana," Amalfi replied.

The door to Dana's office gave a slight creak as she pushed it open, revealing a compact room lined with more bookshelves and a small wooden desk by the window. Mementos from her past travels and photographs decorated the walls. The room had an intimate feel to it, accented by a small jade plant soaking in the dappled sunlight by the window.

Courtney stepped in behind her, gently closing the door. The slight hum of the computer and the A/C could be heard in the background.

"You're going to check the security footage, aren't you?" Courtney asked accusingly as she leaned against the closed door.

Dana nodded, her fingers quickly dancing over the keyboard. "I want to see these people for myself. Maybe we can get a better understanding of what they're up to."

"Okay, Big Brother," Courtney said. Dana ignored her.

The screen flickered to life, displaying the security camera feeds. Dana clicked on a folder labeled "Yesterday" and scrolled to the time when they were in the store according to Amalfi. There they were: six individuals, moving with purpose through the aisles. The footage was clear, revealing their features and mannerisms. It was the same group from the restaurant.

Four men, two women. The tall, bald man with the bird tattoo Amalfi had described was easily distinguishable, leading the pack, pointing out specific books and maps. The others seemed to be in a rush, grabbing what they could and looking over their shoulders nervously.

A woman with red hair was looking at a book on Costa Rican birds, while a man with a hipster beard stood next to the redhead and kept checking his watch.

Leaving the bookstore, Courtney insisted those people were just ordinary tourists out to birdwatch. Dana wasn't so sure about that.

CHAPTER SEVEN

THE NEXT MORNING, DANA AND COURTNEY WALKED toward Big Mike's surf kiosk right on the beach. The crisp morning air was turning thicker, a sign of the humidity that would soon envelop them.

Big Mike's main shop was in Ark Row, next to Dana's bookstore. The kiosk beach location made it easy for his customers looking for fun toys like personal watercraft carriers and snorkeling gear to take into the water. He lined up the toys right on the shore in front of his kiosk, ready to tempt the beach goers into more active fun than laying on a beach towel on the sand.

"Hey, girl," Big Mike greeted Dana. "What can I help you with?"

"Jet skis," Dana said, smiling.

"Two jet skis?" Big Mike said, looking at Courtney.

"That's right," Dana said.

Big Mike grinned widely. "No problem." Though nicknamed Big Mike, he was actually a scrawny man with frosted hair tips right out of a 90s boy band and a deep leathery tan from a lifetime under the sun.

He walked them over to the Kawasaki Jet Skis he had out on

the sand and gave them a quick run-through on how to operate the machines. "Not our first rodeo with these suckers," Dana said with a smile. Big Mike held up his hands in mock surrender.

"Let's get you in the water, then," he said.

Big Mike and his employee, Carlitos Moreno, helped them get into their life vests, then they pushed the machines into the shimmering waves. The powerful hum of the jet skis resonated along with the crashing of the waves as the two women revved up the engines and sped off toward the open water.

Mariposa Beach sat in a mini bay, which made its waters rather gentle compared to other beach towns nearby. But once you made it into the open water, it got rough and choppy in a hurry.

Dana felt the wind rush past her, the spray of the saltwater lightly misting her face. Every time she throttled up, she felt a surge of adrenaline. The vast expanse of the Pacific Ocean stretched out before them. Seemingly endless.

Courtney, riding her own jet ski alongside Dana, let out a joyous whoop, her blonde hair flying behind her as she jumped waves with her jet ski.

For a few minutes, they simply enjoyed the thrill of jet skiing in the ocean, making broad arcs and sharp turns, laughing, and challenging each other with mini races.

The world's worries momentarily faded away as the beauty of nature and the exhilaration of speed took over.

But Dana had a mission in mind. She angled her jet ski toward Morpho Bay, the small inlet at the bottom of that huge cliff in Lapa Mountain where Tino's house was located.

Courtney followed her closely. The ocean's waves grew choppier as they approached the rocky outcroppings near the base of the cliffs. From this vantage point, the height of Tino's cliff house was even more awe-inspiring.

Navigating carefully, Dana slowed down, her eyes scanning the beach below Tino's house. The tide was low, revealing a stretch of sandy shore punctuated by rocks and tide pools. There wasn't any sign of a speedboat or anything out of the ordinary, just the mesmerizing dance of the waves on the shore.

Courtney pulled up next to her, shielding her eyes from the sun. "Everything looks peaceful from here," she commented.

"Yeah," Dana murmured, "but looks can be deceiving. Let's hang around for a bit and see if anything seems amiss."

They cut the engines, letting the gentle waves rock their jet ski.

THE SOUND of roaring engines shattered the stillness of the moment they had been enjoying.

Dana shielded her eyes with her hand as she looked toward the sound of the engines. "There! Two boats," Dana said excitedly, pointing at the source of the ruckus.

From the nook of the cove and its adjoining pebble-laden beach, tucked beneath the vertiginous cliff upon which Tino's charming cottage stood sentinel, a pair of boats burst forth. They churned the placid waters, their motors purring like twin alley cats eager for a fight as they made a beeline toward the open sea.

The sun reflected off the two boats' sleek hulls; their engines roared and churned the water into frothy wakes as they continued their perilous chase. The onshore wind carried shouts and cries, further enhancing the tension of the unfolding scene.

One boat looked like the one they had seen yesterday from the top of the cliff side that made Tino run off to confront it. That boat was being chased by a smaller boat.

"Are they racing?" Courtney asked.

"Doesn't seem like a friendly race to me. Looks like a chase," Dana said.

They watched as the pursuing boat was almost parallel to the other, and Dana could see a male figure on its deck, seemingly preparing to jump from one boat to another. But he didn't jump. Instead, he raised a long stick. For a moment, Dana thought it was a fishing rod or a speargun.

"He has a rifle," Courtney said, panic in her voice.

"And he's aiming it at the other..."

Before Dana could finish the sentence, she heard the crack of gunfire, confirming that the stick was no fishing rod or speargun but a rifle. And the man was aiming and shooting at the pursuing boat.

"Oh, my goodness! He's shooting at him," Courtney said, sounding terrified.

"We need to get closer," Dana said.

"Are you nuts? We need to get the heck out of dodge before they shoot at us," Courtney said.

The waves were choppy, and the breeze had picked up. The two women cautiously advanced, trying to keep to a safe distance while attempting to discern the situation.

Suddenly, another gunshot rang out, echoing across the bay. Dana and Courtney exchanged horrified looks. The urgency of the moment crystallized in their minds.

"We have to help, but without putting ourselves in direct danger," Dana shouted, her eyes scanning the horizon for any other potential allies. "Maybe we can create a diversion or draw attention to the scene. The more eyes are on them, the less likely they'll carry on like this," Dana said.

"Or they'll just shoot us for sticking our nose in whatever is going on there," Courtney said.

It was surreal how in an instant the beauty of the day had

given way to a dramatic and dangerous scene, and both women were now riveted to see how events would play out.

It wouldn't take long.

Dana was trying to figure out what to do next without getting shot when she heard another crack from the rifle. She looked at the boat chasing the other one. The man visibly shuddered, his body recoiling before he succumbed to the embrace of the waters below.

"Oh, no," Dana said, horrified. But it got worse. There was a thundering boom, and then a ball of fire emanated from the boat.

The explosion's shockwave rocked the waters, sending Dana and Courtney swaying on their jet skis, struggling to maintain balance. Fiery fragments and thick plumes of black smoke ascended high into the azure sky, momentarily blocking out the sun.

Dana's heart raced as she instinctively shielded her face with her arm, squinting against the bright flash and heat. The salty sting of the ocean mist, combined with the smoky scent of the explosion, overwhelmed her senses.

Courtney shouted, her voice nearly drowned out by the rumbling aftermath of the explosion, "Dana! Are you okay?"

Though her ears rang, and her vision blurred slightly, Dana nodded. "I'm fine. But that man!" she exclaimed, pointing toward the figure floating in the water amidst the debris. Dana watched the other boat hightail it in the opposite direction.

The man in the water struggled weakly, trying to stay afloat. Without hesitation, Dana gunned her jet ski in his direction, with Courtney after her. As they approached, they could see the man's face was contorted in pain, his clothes singed, and his hair matted from the blast. Dana had expected to see Tino in the water, but she didn't recognize this person. Still, he needed help, urgently, and they were the ones there.

Courtney reached for him first, leaning over and extending her hand. "Hold on!"

They pulled the injured man onto the back of Dana's jet ski, positioning him between the seat and the rear handle, which he clutched weakly.

"We need to get back to shore and get him to a hospital," Dana shouted over the engine's roar, her eyes darting to the other boat; it was long gone. "The nearest hospital is thirty miles from here."

"What do we do?"

"Let's take him to that beach," Dana said, looking at the small bay beneath the towering cliff where Tino's house was perched.

Courtney nodded. They aimed the nose of the jet skis toward the shore and gunned it. Courtney hung back in the diagonal just in case the wounded man fell off Dana's jet ski.

As Dana and Courtney sped towards the shore, the wind whipped around them; the sound of the jet ski engines competed with the roaring waves. The injured man clung to Dana's back, his grip weak but determined. Every so often, a groan of pain would escape his lips, but he held on.

Dana could feel the weight and heat of him, a constant reminder of the gravity of their situation. Her heart raced, not just from adrenaline but also from a responsibility towards this injured stranger. Every so often she would glance back, ensuring he was still with them, and she would see Courtney's focused eyes mirroring her own concern.

The shore approached quickly, a welcoming stretch of sandy refuge within a cove. With practiced ease, Dana and Courtney angled their jet skis, skimming smoothly over the last of the rolling waves and sliding up onto the sand. The wet sand sprayed around them as the powerful machines came to a stop.

Almost immediately, the injured man's grip loosened, and

he crumpled, sliding off the back of the jet ski and onto the soft beach below. Dana and Courtney quickly dismounted, rushing to his side.

Dana kneeled, gently turning him over to inspect his injuries. His face was pale and his breathing ragged. Dark, scorched marks marred his clothing, evidence of the boat's explosion.

"He needs help, badly," Courtney said, her tone urgent.

Dana was already on it, pulling out her phone. "No signal!"

Courtney quickly checked her own device. "Same here."

Dana looked around the deserted inlet trying to decide what to do with the injured man when she heard a voice that made her shudder.

CHAPTER EIGHT

THE SHORE AT THE COVE WAS A SMALL, SHELTERED BEACH about five hundred feet long. The injured man was lying on the gritty pebbled sand, unconscious.

Dana was relieved to see the voice that had made her jump ten feet in the air belonged to an older, stocky woman who was walking towards them.

As the woman approached them, a small boat that looked like a canoe with an outboard motor on it pulled onto the beach. A sun-weathered man with curly black hair and stubble exited the boat, and he too made his way toward them. There was a look of concern on both faces.

"Who are they?" Courtney asked.

Dana shrugged. "No idea, but that explosion was loud, so it must have gotten their attention." She looked out at the wreckage of the boat, still burning in the water.

The woman, her cheeks flushed from rushing over, said her name was Daniela and that she lived in a farmhouse nearby.

"That explosion echoed right through my kitchen as I was sorting beans. I could see the flames from my kitchen window," she explained, her eyes darting towards the unconscious man. "Is he dead?"

"No, he's still breathing," Dana said.

The man said his name was Inigo and that he was a lobster and crab fisherman. His craggy face served as a testament to years under the sun in that profession.

"I was nearby, pulling in my lobster traps, when the sound of the explosion reached me. I rushed over just in time to see you two rescuing him," he gestured toward the injured man with a hint of admiration at Dana and Courtney's action.

"Rub his hands, it'll help circulation," Inigo said. Then he glanced at the stranger's boots and added, "We need to get those boots off him. They'll be filled with water."

"We tried to call 911, but we couldn't get a signal," Dana said.

"Those phones won't work out here," Inigo said.

"I called the police from my landline back home before coming down. I told them there was a boat explosion in the water. That should get them out here faster than usual," Daniela said.

Dana looked down at the injured man. She thought it would be Tino, but it wasn't him. Perhaps the long-time locals knew him. "Do you know who he is?" Dana asked, looking at Daniela and Inigo. They shook their heads.

"Never seen him, so he must not be from around here," Daniela said. "If he was local, I would know him."

The man they had rescued was a puzzle. He was not dressed like your typical boater; he looked more like a workman prepared for a long day's labor. The sturdy pants and the black shirt, combined with those hiking boots, seemed out of place for someone on a boat in those waters, under the sizzling tropical sun.

Following Inigo's advice, Dana and Courtney kneeled by

the unconscious man and rubbed his cold, wet hands, urging life back into them. Inigo removed the man's boots and tipped them over, and sure enough they were filled with water.

"It's going to be a while before help arrives," Dana said, looking around the beach. "Can an ambulance even get down here?"

"No. The main road is about a mile back there, near my farm. But there are thick trees and brush between the road and the beach," Daniela explained.

Dana wasn't sure about the rubbing of the hands, but the stranger's demeanor seemed to improve as she and Courtney rubbed his hands, which felt warmer than when they'd started. The color was returning to his pale face, and his breathing became more regular. A faint murmur escaped his lips, then slowly his eyes fluttered open, revealing a deep confusion at finding the four of them looking down at him.

"Where...where am I?" His voice was weak but filled with a perplexing mix of dread and relief.

"You're safe now," Dana comforted him, her voice soothing. He looked familiar to Dana, but she couldn't place him.

The stranger's gaze traveled from face to face, finally stopping at Dana. He seemed to try to piece together his memories. "Lobo... it was Lobo. He did this to me," he whispered with a grimace, anger seeping into his voice.

Dana looked at Daniela and Inigo. The name of Lobo sent a visible shiver down their spines, and put fear into their eyes.

There was much more to this story, but the stranger slipped back into unconsciousness.

Then Dana noticed a streak of blood seeping out of the injured man's mouth. "He's bleeding from the inside," Inigo said ominously. The fisherman kneeled and turned the man on his side to look at his back. A large crimson stain covered the back of the stranger's shirt. Inigo recoiled.

"He's been shot!" Inigo exclaimed, his voice taking on an edge of terror. He scrambled back from the injured man, looking around frantically, as if expecting danger to pounce from any corner.

"We saw a man on the other boat firing a rifle at him," Dana said.

"Was that Lobo?" Courtney wondered.

The name 'Lobo' seemed to act like a switch that turned off every trace of compassion in Inigo. His once helpful eyes now darted around the beach with a wild fear. "Lobo will be back," Inigo said softly. As if he were talking to himself. Without another word to the group, he began a hasty retreat towards his boat.

Dana jumped to her feet, chasing after him. "Where are you going? We need your help."

Inigo didn't break his pace. Nor did he turn to face Dana. His voice quivered as he walked away. "If Lobo did this, he won't let it reach the police. He has eyes everywhere. He will make sure no evidence or witnesses remain. You're in danger if you stay here."

"We can't leave him!" Dana protested, her voice straining with desperation. "We need to help him."

"Suit yourself," he murmured. "But I've seen what Lobo and his men are capable of. If you value your life and the lives of your friends, you'll leave now."

Inigo pushed his boat back into the water and leaped inside, reaching for the chord of the outboard motor. With one swift pull, the engine roared to life, drowning out Dana's protests. Making a sharp turn, he steered the boat into the vast expanse of the Pacific, leaving behind a trail of churning water and the smell of gasoline. Dana stood there, stunned.

She made her way back to Courtney and Daniela, who were looking after the stranger.

Courtney's voice trembled. "That was... intense. Just who is this Lobo?"

Dana, processing everything, shook her head. "I've got no idea. Doña Daniela, is Lobo someone you're familiar with?"

Doña Daniela took a deep breath, her eyes darkening. "Yes, I've heard of him. There are... incidents here sometimes. Criminals. They find this area to be a quiet space for their... dastardly transactions. No witness out here, as you can see."

"Until today. We're all witnesses," Courtney said shakily.

"Do you have anyone nearby who might help? Family, neighbors?" Dana asked.

"My husband and our grandson are in town at our pulperia in Plano Azul. It's a good ten miles from here. The closest person I can think of is Tino, right up on that cliff." Daniela pointed at the house perched above them like an enormous gargoyle from Gothic architecture.

If Tino was home, he would help. But she couldn't see how to get to his place from here. It must be a good two hundred feet up.

"I don't think Tino is around, though," Daniela said.

"How can you tell from down here?"

"He usually has his boat moored in that cove cave right over there. I don't see it," Daniela said.

Dana's gaze drifted out to the bay, where remnants of the exploded boat were still visible. A shared realization dawned between Dana and Courtney.

"Could that have been Tino's boat?" Courtney whispered, an edge of panic in her voice. "And if it was, then who is this man? Why was he on Tino's boat, being chased by someone as menacing as Lobo?"

Before they could reflect on that notion, they heard in the distance the sound of a boat's engine. And it was growing louder, as if it were heading their way. Dana couldn't see it.

"It's Lobo! He's coming back to finish him off, and get rid of us, witnesses," Courtney said, sounding like she was on the edge of panic.

Daniela made the sign of the cross.

Dana wanted to calm her friend down and reassure her, but she feared she might be right. The engine kept getting louder. Whoever that was, the boat would be visible soon. And if Dana could see them, they would be able to see her.

CHAPTER NINE

THE SHIP CAME INTO THE SMALL INLET AND INTO FULL view. To her relief, it wasn't Lobo. Nor a regular boat you saw every day in Mariposa Beach. It was a large cutter with a huge Costa Rican flag flapping in the wind. It was the Costa Rican Coast Guard!

"Oh, thank goodness!" Courtney sighed in relief, her posture softening a little.

Dana watched in awe as the cutter approached and parted the waves with authority. The coastguard men could help the wounded stranger.

Daniela looked at the ship with pride. Dana supposed her 911 call about a boat explosion had gotten them over quickly. She was relieved that Daniela had done that, but she hadn't expected the Coast Guard to show up.

She figured Officer Freddy would drive up on his motocross bike, eventually. This show of force was a sight to sore eyes. If Lobo was around, there was no way he would dare stick around now.

The stark white cutter stood in contrast to the blue of the ocean, and the red, white, and blue of the Costa Rican flag danced with each gust of wind. Its side boldly printed with the word GUARDACOSTAS — Coast Guard in Spanish — reassured the three women that they were safe, and the stranger would get the help he desperately needed. Dana prayed it wasn't too late.

The cutter pulled up to the shipwreck. Dana waved her arms as she called out to the cutter as if she were shipwrecked, pleading to be rescued. A minute later, a smaller dinghy equipped with an outboard motor was lowered from the cutter's port side, its propeller churning the water into foam as it made its way toward the beach. Dana could see four Coast Guardsmen in uniform on the dinghy.

"Hang on just a bit longer," Dana whispered to the wounded man, patting his hand gently. "Help is coming." The wounded man was still unconscious, so no reply came from him.

As she watched the dingy approach, the cutter inspected the wreckage on the water. Way off in the distance, Dana saw Inigo's small boat as it vanished on the other side of a rock formation.

Courtney's brow furrowed in suspicion. She had been watching Inigo's boat, too. "Do you think he's involved in all this? Why would he run away like that?"

"I don't think so. He was as helpful as he could be until the mention of Lobo. I think he ran away in fear of Lobo, not the authorities," Dana said.

"I guess he's more scared of Lobo than of leaving the scene of a crime," Courtney said. That sent a shiver down Dana's spine. It spoke volumes of the fear this man Lobo had around these parts.

"We'll have to let the Coast Guard know about Inigo and Lobo. The Coast Guard might be able to provide us with information about Lobo's identity and why he is feared," Dana said.

Within moments, the dinghy glided onto the sand; the

guardsmen stepped out and secured it. A guardsman stood with the dinghy as the three others approached Dana and the others. One of the men was holding a first aid kit, and he went right to work on the injured man. He waved a small flask of smelling salt under the man's nose to restore consciousness. The stranger's eyes fluttered open sporadically, disorientation apparent on his face as he tried to make sense of his surroundings. The guardsman quickly administered first aid and began stabilizing him.

"What happened out here?" the guardsman asked Dana. He was in his forties and seemed in charge. That's when Dana noticed the other guardsman next to the older one was a woman.

Dana explained what had happened.

"None of you know this man?" he asked.

All three women shook their heads.

The female guardsman kneeled next to the stranger, who now had an oxygen tube clipped to his nostrils and an IV bag in his arm.

"Can you hear me?" she asked the wounded man.

The stranger managed a nod, his voice coming out as a mere whisper.

"Who shot you?"

The man swallowed hard but said nothing.

"What's your name?"

A pregnant pause followed, during which the stranger seemed to weigh his options. "Garcia," he finally responded.

Dana and Courtney exchanged glances, sensing the hesitancy in his voice.

"Care to tell us why someone wanted you dead?" the coast guardsman in charge asked.

Garcia's gaze fell. "Please, don't ask. Just... thank you for saving me, but I can't say anything right now."

Seeing the wounded man's hesitation, the coast guardsman gave a resigned sigh. "We're going to need answers, Garcia." But before he could press further, two other guardsmen approached with a stretcher, carefully transferring Garcia onto it.

Dana then heard a motocross bike. She turned to see an officer with the National Police tearing through the rough terrain right onto the beach. The officer leaned the bike on its kickstand and removed his helmet. Dana was relieved to see the friendly face of Officer Freddy Sanchez.

For the next thirty minutes, he took statements from Dana, Courtney, and Daniela, keen to piece together the mysterious events.

The guardsmen had taken the stranger going by the name of Garcia back to the big ship. A few minutes later, Dana saw a helicopter taking off from the cutter, hovering above the ship before taking off toward the city. It was quite impressive.

Dana turned her attention back to Officer Freddy. Daniela was telling him about Inigo, emphasizing his hasty retreat upon hearing the name of Lobo.

"I know Inigo. He is a known lobster poacher, but small scale. Sells them himself at the market in Nosara. Unless you're a lobster, he's harmless," Officer Freddy said. "He probably didn't want to get in trouble for his illegal catch of the day."

"What about the name Lobo? The injured man said Lobo shot him, and Inigo turned white like a sheet upon hearing that name," Dana said.

"Lobo? Now he's not harmless," Officer Freddy said. "He's a known leader of an illegal fishing and wildlife smuggling outfit."

"What is happening in Mariposa Bay?" Dana asked, trying to connect the dots. It shattered her naivety when she found out about the criminal dark side that existed down there.

The lone coast guardsman who had remained behind sighed. "You might not see it, but the smuggling activities around here are getting worse. It's gone from a lone poacher like Inigo to these big criminal organizations connected to the cartels."

"Yes, many unfamiliar motorboats have been frequenting the bay lately," Daniela said."It's unsettling to hear the late-night boat activities."

Dana's eyes widened. "What are they smuggling?"

"Anything that turns a profit is fair game," the guardsman said.

"Is it possible Garcia works for Lobo? They had a falling out?" Dana ventured.

The coast guardsman simply shrugged. "Could be. Until he's ready to talk, we can only speculate. But given what we saw today, nothing would surprise me."

"What happens to him now?" Courtney asked.

"They'll fix him up in the hospital, then he'll be questioned by the OIJ."

"I hope Tino is okay," Dana said, looking up at his house on the cliff.

"Doesn't look like he's around. He missed all the action, practically right under his nose," Officer Freddy said.

Dana laughed, realizing it had been a while since she'd had something to laugh about. She wanted to check on Tino but wasn't sure how to get all the way up that cliff. And they'd been gone for almost three hours now — Big Mike would be worried sick about his jet skis. And them.

"We better head back to Mariposa Beach, before Big Mike reports those jet skis as stolen," Dana said. Courtney's eyes widened. "I'm kidding, Court. He wouldn't do that. But he is probably worried about us."

"And just ditch this saga of a blown-up boat, a mystery man shot, and the notorious smuggler, Lobo, out there? Well, when you put it like that, how can I refuse? Lead the way back to Mariposa Beach. I need a banana daiquiri!" Courtney said.

With the green light from the coast guardsmen and Officer Freddy to leave, Dana gave Danila a hug and thanked her for her help, and for calling 911. Dana and Courtney made their way to the jet skis as the dinghy returned to the beach to pick up their boss. Two young guardsmen jumped out to help them get their jet skis back out on the water as Courtney batted her eyelashes playfully. "Thanks, gentlemen," she said, her voice dripping with charm as the two girls revved up the engines and sped off toward Mariposa Beach, riding side by side.

Dana chuckled. "Flirting with the coast guard. Really, Court?"

Courtney smirked. "What can I say? Cute guys in uniform are my kryptonite."

CHAPTER TEN

As Dana and Courtney approached the sandy shores of Mariposa Beach, the familiar landmarks offered Dana a sense of security that had been missing for the past few hours. Even from a distance, the silhouettes of Big Mike and his young assistant, Carlitos, were unmistakable. They stood by the beach kiosk, looking out at the horizon as if anticipating their return.

Dana throttled down her jet ski, creating a gentle arc towards the beach, and Courtney followed suit. As the jet skis roared and the water splashed around them, the hum of the engines gave way to the familiar sounds of Mariposa Beach — laughing children, waves gently breaking, and distant chatter from the Que Vista restaurant and from Ark Row nearby.

They glided onto the beach, the hulls of their jet skis scraping softly against the wet sand. Before Dana could even turn off the engine, Big Mike was there to steady the watercraft.

"Got yourself into another adventure, did ya?" Mike boomed with a mix of mock frustration and genuine relief. Carlitos, wiry and swift, had already reached Courtney's jet ski, giving her a hand as she disembarked.

Wiping the sea spray off her face, Dana let out an exhausted laugh. "You won't believe half of it, Mike."

Mike gave a hearty laugh, his eyes crinkling at the corners. "Oh, I've seen plenty in my time here. But nothing that takes three hours with a mystery man shot up, a boat blowing up, and the Coast Guard coming to the rescue. Trouble finds you, Dana, like a dog finds a puddle right after a bath."

Dana couldn't believe it. The jet ski was still warm, and word of her adventure had already reached Big Mike and Mariposa Beach.

"Geez, even for Mariposa Beach, word got out fast," Dana said.

"Thanks for these beasts, Mike. They held up well. And thanks for being understanding about us being gone so long with them."

"They are beauts, aren't they?" Big Mike said, sounding like a proud papa. "And no worries. I'm mighty impressed you could pluck that dude from the water without a rescue board or even a towline."

"I guess we got lucky," Dana said, looking at Courtney.

Carlitos began securing the jet skis as Mike turned to Dana, his expression suddenly more serious. "You always get out of these types of jams in one piece. That's all I care about. But remember, kiddo, life ain't a movie. Especially with the likes of Lobo in the picture. Be careful out there."

"You know Lobo?" Dana asked excitedly.

"I know of him. And his bad reputation. I've never met the dude. Hope I never do."

A small crowd of onlookers had gathered around Big Mike's kiosk as Dana and Courtney made their way off the beach.

"Why is everyone staring at us?" Courtney asked.

"Word travels fast in a small beach town," Big Mike said.

"Ugh," Courtney said, blowing a strand of hair away from her face.

"Welcome to Mariposa Beach," Dana said, smiling.

Doña Luz and Doña Chila watched them from a red painted concrete bench on the sidewalk. As soon as Dana got within earshot, the barrage of questions began.

"Who was that man that was shot up and blown up, Dana?" Doña Chila asked, wide-eyed.

"I don't know, Doña Chila. That's up to the authorities to figure out," Dana said as they walked by the bench without stopping to engage with the old biddies of the Gossip Brigade.

As they crossed Main Street toward Ark Row, Dana could hear Doña Amada derisively tell Doña Chilla: "Told you she wouldn't know anything good." Dana didn't acknowledge the comment, nor did she turn back to the old ladies. She just kept walking toward her bookstore.

Ark Row's boardwalk was usually a calm boulevard of quaint little shops: the jewelry store, Big Mike's surf shop, and Dana's bookstore "slash" café, apart from an ice cream parlor. Every shop owner seemed to be outside their storefronts, eyes darting to Dana and Courtney as they walked by. "I feel like an animal on display at the zoo," Courtney said.

"Oh, look! It's them!" Mrs. Segura, the local florist, discreetly pointed in their direction with a bouquet in her hands.

As they approached the bookstore, the familiar wooden sign of Dana's bookstore swung gently in the wind. The painted letters spelling "Books, Bagels, and Coffee" glinted in the setting sun. A couple of regular customers who were sitting outside sipping their coffees gave them supportive nods.

Amalfi quickly pushed open the door for them. "Wild day, huh?" she remarked, as the bell above the door tinkled. She hugged Dana right at the door.

"You could say that," Dana replied, grateful for the sanctuary of her store.

Though many patrons looked up, it was Mindy behind the counter who froze in her tracks, wearing her characteristic apron splattered with remnants of the day's pastries. Mindy's warm hazel eyes filled with emotion upon seeing Dana.

"Oh my gosh, Dana!" Without hesitation, Mindy hurriedly handed a coffee pot to her husband Leo and dashed out from behind the counter.

Dana, taken aback by the sudden attention, barely had a moment to react before she was enveloped in a tight, warm embrace.

"So you heard?" Dana asked.

"The entire district has heard by now," Mindy said. "I was so worried about you, and your phone kept going straight to voicemail."

"No cell signal out there. But, yes, it was... quite a day. But we're okay."

Courtney stood there awkwardly. She was Dana's best friend from her old life in San Francisco, and Mindy had seemingly replaced her. *Mindy is the tropical me*, Courtney thought.

Mindy cupped Dana's face gently. "You always find yourself in these wild situations, don't you? Promise me you'll be more careful?"

Dana chuckled softly. "I promise. Today was enough excitement for a while."

"Famous last words," Courtney said with a smirk.

Mindy laughed, knowing no one could rein in Dana when she was onto something. Like a dog with a bone, she would not let go.

Dana glanced around her store, comforted by the familiar sight of worn-out leather chairs, the old grandfather clock ticking softly, and stacks of books that promised adventures far removed from the day's events.

She felt bad for Courtney. Her friend had come out here to have a fun vacation and relax away from her busy San Francisco life, but Dana had ruined it by dragging her on crazy adventures. "I'm sorry for messing up your vacation, Court," Dana said.

"Hey, I came down to spend time with you. We're doing plenty of that. But, yeah, let's ease up being front and center to shootings, explosions, smugglers known as Lobo, and a Coast Guard rescue," Courtney said. "Well, I liked the Coast Guard part. They were cute."

The two friends shared another laugh, reveling in the normalcy of their surroundings. Today had been unexpected and overwhelming, but Dana knew there was a long way to go before getting to the bottom of the dark clouds that had gathered over Tino's house. She kept on wondering, *just where the heck had Tino vanished to?*

CHAPTER ELEVEN

Dana stepped through the door of her home, a wave of relief washing over her. The familiar walls and trinkets were an immediate comfort after the day's harrowing adventure. And her cat, Wally, rubbing against her legs and purring, put her at ease.

Though the threat of the enigmatic Lobo loomed large in Dana's mind, she downplayed the danger. Would Lobo really come after them? Seemed doubtful, since neither she nor Courtney had any clue about the boat clash or the tension between Lobo and Garcia. She didn't even know if it had been Lobo on the other boat shooting at Garcia. The injured man said it was Lobo, but she wouldn't be able to pick him out of a line-up without seeing his face. It seemed like an unnecessary risk for Lobo to take. Maybe, she mused, the whole scenario was less about smuggling and more about some maritime feud. After all, road rage was ubiquitous — why not sea rage?

Regardless of her theories, Dana felt gross at the uncomfortable grit of sand sticking to her skin and the pungent mix of seawater and sweat that seemed to cling to her after spending hours exposed to the elements.

Even Wally gave her a disdainful look after taking in a whiff of her body odor before darting away. Eager to wash the day away, she shed her sandy clothes and indulged in a warm shower.

Dressed in a soft pastel-colored tunic and comfy shorts, Dana padded down to the kitchen. Courtney, her usually bubbly friend, seemed deep in thought. The light chatter of their shared experience echoed in the room.

"Hey," Dana said softly, approaching Courtney.

Courtney looked up, offering a slight smile. "Quite an adventure today, huh?"

"Yeah," Dana responded. "What we need right now is a pitcher of banana daiquiri."

"Now you're talking," Courtney said.

Dana got to work, and in no time the countertop was littered with a cutting board, ripe bananas, a bottle of white rum, a bucket of ice, and a blender.

"Do you remember how to make this?" Dana asked, peeling a banana.

Courtney smirked. "How hard can it be? Bananas, rum, some ice, and a dash of sugar, right?"

"And a splash of lime juice for that Costa Rica tang," Dana corrected with a smile.

Courtney playfully rolled her eyes. "Of course, the secret ingredient."

As they worked, Wally jumped onto the kitchen counter, his curious green eyes darting from one ingredient to another.

Courtney chuckled. "Looks like someone's interested."

"Hey, you, off the counter." Dana waved a hand gently at Wally. "You can watch, but no helping today. Besides, it's just bananas up here — no meat, silly."

Wally meowed in protest but jumped down, settling on a nearby stool, still eyeing the bananas with interest.

With the blender humming, the kitchen was soon filled with the sweet aroma of banana daiquiri. Pouring the creamy concoction into two glasses, Dana raised hers. "To unexpected adventures and their much-needed aftermath."

Courtney clinked her glass against Dana's, smiling, "And to the best company to have them with." Wally meowed in agreement as they made their way upstairs and outside to the veranda. They sat down in the comfy chaise lounges out on the deck. They sipped their drinks, the cool, fruity blend providing a stark contrast to the day's heated events.

Dana sighed, leaning back, "You know, I've been thinking..."

"About?"

"Why would they come after us? We know nothing."

Courtney pondered that for a moment, her fingers playing with the rim of her glass. "I guess it's the not knowing part that's got me spooked. Movies and crime shows always have that one innocent bystander who gets dragged into things."

"Well, let's hope our lives are less dramatic than a movie plot. But, really, they have no reason to bother with us. We're just two bystanders who happened to be in the wrong place at the wrong time."

They sat in comfortable silence for a while, absorbing the tranquility of the evening.

"I'm glad we're here, though," Courtney finally said, her voice filled with gratitude. "This place, this moment... it's healing. San Francisco gets a bit much. This is a nice break from the city, even though there might be a smuggler named Lobo after us."

Benny arrived an hour later and joined them on the veranda with a glass of daiquiri. Dana and Courtney told him about their wild adventure.

"Wow! You saved the fellow's life. And it looks as though

you've stumbled on a mysterious bit of business in that motor-boat chase. What did the man say his name was?"

"Garcia," Dana answered doubtfully. "Sounds like a fake name to me."

"Of course—there are lots of Garcias in the world. It might be his real name. But more than likely it isn't. Did he give his first name?" Benny pursued.

"No. Just Garcia."

"Would he tell you anything about the reason for the chase? Did you question him?"

"He wouldn't tell us anything at all. We made a few inquiries, but he said he couldn't explain."

"Still more mysterious," reflected Benny.

"He was a bit out of it after the explosion and getting shot," Dana said.

"Do you think he will talk to the police when he gets better?" Courtney asked.

"I'm afraid not. He seemed quite determined not to tell us anything about himself or about the men who were chasing him."

"Before he clammed up, right after we got him out of the water, he said Lobo did this. After mentioning Lobo, the lobster fisherman freaked out and took off. Told them Lobo was a dangerous man. Have you ever heard of a smuggler named Lobo?"

"Lobo! Sure, everyone who grew up around here knows about Lobo. He's a well-known figure."

"Who is he?" asked Dana.

"Jaime Lobo is a noted criminal. He is a poacher — the leader of a ring of smugglers who poaches turtle eggs and wildlife up and down the coast."

"That's what Tino said when he had seen a boat out there. He said they were poachers and took off," Dana said.

"You think they mixed Tino up in this?" Benny asked.

"I don't know for sure. But there is one way to find out," Dana replied as Courtney and Benny looked at her with furrowed brows.

"You want to go back there? Don't you?" Benny asked.

Before Dana could reply, Courtney guffawed at the mention of going back. "Twice we've been near the vicinity of Tino's place, and we've been attacked with a machete and seen a wild boat chase and shooting right out of Miami Vice. And you want to go back there?"

Dana smiled. "Yup."

CHAPTER TWELVE

BENNY DROVE HIS SUV WITH DANA IN THE PASSENGER seat and Courtney in the back. She reminded Dana this was a bad idea a few times during the forty-minute drive up to Tino's place.

They had taken the main road rather than the off-road path Dana had chosen before, so it was a longer drive but much less perilous, though the two-lane blacktop asphalt snaking up the twisty mountainside was narrow and full of potholes.

"During the rainy season, this road is even worse. It's slick, and there are muddy landslides that end up shutting it down for months," Benny said.

Tino's sudden disappearance baffled Dana, although Benny and Courtney weren't sure he had disappeared. Even Officer Freddy had dismissed that concern. "He lives alone, and he's eccentric. It's only been a couple of days. He'll show up," Freddy had said.

Finally, Benny pulled onto a gravel road that led up to a wooden gate. A "no trespassing" private property sign was tacked on the gate. "No doorbell?" Courtney said, looking around.

"I could honk," Benny said.

"Not if Lobo is hanging around there," Courtney said.

"Well, it's a simple gate. And we drove all the way out here," Benny said.

Tino had crafted a straightforward gate design by wrapping a length of steel wire at the top and bottom of the fence post across from the gate opening. He had used fencing staples to fasten the wire in place. The lower end of the gatepost was carefully inserted into the waiting loop at the base, as though it were unlocking a secret passage.

Benny got out of the car. He walked to the gate and with a stretch and pull that released the hook's tension, the upper end of the gate post came loose, allowing him to swing the gate open.

"Great. We won't honk in case Lobo the smuggler is in there, but we're ignoring the no-trespass sign and just driving right on in," Courtney said, laying the sarcasm on thick.

Benny slowly drove up the gravel driveway. It was about fifty feet before they saw a barn, a large shed, and the house.

"I was expecting a rundown place. This is nice," Benny said.

"I was surprised about that too when he brought us here," Dana said.

"His truck is gone," Courtney said.

Benny parked, and they got out of the SUV. Chickens darted around while a pair of Tino's goats eyed them skeptically. The unmistakable bark of Tino's dog, Ringo, echoed from within the house.

"You think he's got one of those ferocious farm dogs?" Benny inquired at Ringo's persistent barking.

"He's a marshmallow," Dana chuckled. "Met him yesterday."

The farm had an eerie stillness. Dana peered through a window. The disarray inside was alarming. It pointed to signs of a struggle.

They called for Tino but were met with silence. When Dana tried the door, it swung open; she was expecting it to be locked.

"Maybe he doesn't need to lock up out here in the middle of nowhere," Benny said.

Ringo came running toward her, paws to her chest, tail wagging, tongue licking her face. Dana couldn't help but giggle at the enthusiastic greeting. "Down, Ringo, down," she ordered, and to her surprise he did as instructed. He sat wagging his tail. Then he bounded outside and immediately went potty.

"Poor doggy had to go," Courtney said.

Dana walked inside.

"Dana, wait! We can't just walk in," Courtney protested.

But they had trespassed the second they drove onto Tino's property — and Dana was here to do a wellness check on the old man, not steal anything.

Benny followed Dana inside.

"What a mess," Benny remarked, glancing at the overturned furniture.

A resigned Courtney followed Benny.

Dana tried piecing together what had happened.

"What if Garcia stumbled upon Tino's place, broke in to burgle him, there was a fight, and then the boat chase happened?"

"How did they make it down to the beach from way up here?" Courtney asked.

"And where was Tino?" Benny added.

Dana suddenly saw movement outside. At first, she thought it was Ringo or a goat, but it was a person. "Tino?" she said excitedly, looking out the window. But this person was running fast, and it wasn't Tino.

As Courtney yelled at her to not give chase, Dana was

already running after the figure. Benny took off after Dana. And soon Ringo joined the chase, tail wagging.

The man was fast, and he had already created a hefty gap between them. But he was heading towards the edge of the cliff and running out of room to run. Suddenly, he vanished in a thick brush.

Dana shrieked. "The cliff!" She stopped short as Benny and Courtney joined her. They looked around, puzzled.

"Do you think... he went over?" Courtney said, looking toward the cliff side.

The three of them slowly walked to the edge of the steep cliff. The wind whipped their hair and clothes. Looking down, Dana saw the small inlet and cove below where they had brought the injured Garcia. But she didn't see a body splayed out down there.

"Where the heck did he go?" Dana said, looking around.

"There must be a way down there from here," Benny said. "It's not uncommon for homes up here to have a pathway down to the beach. Maybe that's what happened to our runner. He knows the secret pathway down there."

"Did you recognize him?" Dana said.

Benny nodded.

"Me too. He was the bald man with the tattoo on his head that was hanging around with those so-called birdwatchers at the restaurant and my bookstore," Dana said.

"So what the heck was he doing here? And where's Tino now?" Benny wondered.

"I knew something was not right out here and with those people," Dana said.

"Maybe that was Lobo," Courtney said.

"No, that's not him. Lobo doesn't like his photo taken, but there is one from around ten years ago that the press uses when he makes the news, and that wasn't him. He's older. And he has hair. And Tattoo Head is a white guy, European or American. Lobo is from out here in Guanacaste," Benny said.

"I doubt Lobo would have dinner at Que Vista," Dana added.

"So who is that guy?" Courtney said.

"I don't know, but if he's having dinner at Mariposa Beach and visiting my bookstore, he must be staying near town," Dana said.

Ringo's plaintive whine drew their attention. The dog sat dramatically by the cliff, gazing out at the water like a melancholic hero from a classic novel. "He misses his dad," Dana said as she stooped down to comfort him. That's when she noticed a bright red feather tangled in his collar. Dana plucked the feather and held it up for examination.

"That's unusual," she mused, showing it to Benny and Courtney.

Benny brushed it off. "He probably enjoys chasing birds."

"Tino loved those birds. His dog wouldn't harm them," Dana argued.

They went back toward the house, where they spotted a toppled birdcage on the ground between the house and the aviary. Dana's heart sank as she rushed to the aviary. She found it almost empty compared to just yesterday.

"They're after the parrots," she whispered.

"All this for a bird? Really?" Courtney said.

"Remember what they said. Exotic bird smuggling is big bucks for criminals like Lobo. With that much money, anything can happen," Dana explained, motioning around.

Benny nodded. "Greed can lead people to do unthinkable things."

"I wonder if Garcia is connected with Lobo? They came here to steal the birds. Tino catches them and the fight is on," Courtney said.

"It's plausible, but there is one glaring problem with your theory," Dana said pensively.

"What is it?"

"Garcia was chasing Lobo. Lobo shot him. Remember?"

"Oh yeah," Courtney said.

"Garcia and Lobo could have been in cahoots. They steal the birds together. They fight off Tino. Then, as they're taking the birds, Garcia and Lobo go at it. And then... you know the rest," Benny said.

Dana knitted her eyebrows. "That's interesting. Maybe one of them tried to double-cross the other. No honor among thieves and all that."

"If that is true, I don't think it bodes well for Tino," Courtney said.

Courtney was right. If Tino had confronted Lobo, they might have killed him. Easy enough to get rid of a body up here in the middle of nowhere. They could have buried him somewhere on Tino's property or dumped him in the ocean.

Ringo still looked sadly into the water. Was that where his dad was?

Courtney's voice was cautious, barely above a whisper. "What about the disappearing act? The man who vanished... Mr. Clean. Do you think he's in cahoots with Lobo and Garcia? Could he be a linchpin in this smuggling network?"

Dana's eyes darted around, considering all possibilities. "I don't know, but we need to find out," she said.

"So, what now?" Courtney asked.

"Let's head back to town. Find Mr. Clean," Dana said.

"We have to call the police to report this mess," Benny said, looking around.

"Of course, but we have to wait until we're back in signal range so we can report this mess. The police ought to have an update on Garcia. He must be doing better now, and talking," Dana said.

The trio made their way to Benny's SUV. Ringo, tail wagging with gusto, dashed towards them, leaping effortlessly into the vehicle.

Benny shot the canine a brief, perturbed glance, but couldn't resist the charm of its happily lolling tongue.

"Think we could bring him along? Just until we figure out where Tino is," Dana proposed, her eyes pleading.

Courtney, always practical, chimed in, "And what about the parrots, goats, and chickens?"

"I'll make an exception for one extra passenger, but only of the four-legged and canine variety. Not the entire farm," Benny quipped.

Chuckling, Dana replied, "Don't worry, I'll inform the police about the rest of the animals as soon as I get a signal on my phone."

"And if Tino just comes back from a grocery run, he's gonna think we dognapped Ringo," Courtney said.

Looking down at Ringo, her tone somber, Dana said, "Something tells me Tino won't be returning anytime soon." She hugged the dog close, offering solace to the grieving pet.

CHAPTER THIRTEEN

As the uneven terrain gradually smoothed into the main road to Mariposa Beach, one little bar brightened up as Dana's phone buzzed to life with notices of missed text messages and notifications.

"Finally, a signal!"

Without a second's delay, she dialed Detective Rojas. Detective Jorge Picado was another option, but the mere thought of contacting him made Dana cringe. Their relationship was as amicable as that of a lion with a zebra. She got along with Picado's partner, Gabriela Rojas.

Rojas and Picado were agents with the OIJ, the national police force dedicated to investigating major crimes.

OIJ agents were plainclothes detectives — a mix of a big city detective and an FBI special agent back in the States. Given the gravity of recent events — a man shot, a boat explosion, and Tino's sudden disappearance — the OIJ had taken charge. But Picado? No way Dana was ringing him up.

Rojas answered promptly. Realizing the connection was precarious, Dana wasted no time in detailing the scene at Tino's and her growing suspicion of Lobo's involvement.

"Thank you, Dana," Rojas acknowledged. "I'll certainly look into it."

Curiosity gnawing at her, Dana probed, "Have you questioned Garcia about Lobo?"

A momentary pause ensued before Rojas replied, "I'd have loved to."

Oh, no, Dana thought. Garcia had died.

"What happened? Did he..."

Rojas sighed heavily. "He was alive. But, um... well, Garcia was kidnapped earlier today."

Dana was left reeling. "You're kidding, right?"

"I wish I was," Rojas said.

After Rojas had filled Dana in, the call ended. Dana shook her head in disbelief.

"What happened?" Benny asked. Courtney leaned forward to listen.

"Garcia slipped away from the hospital," Dana began, voice filled with disbelief. "However, he didn't get far. Two hospital guards spotted him being forcibly bundled into a black SUV with darkened windows. By the time they reacted, the vehicle was gone, vanishing into the streets. They do not know who was behind this or where they've taken him."

Benny's grip on the steering wheel tightened, his knuckles turning white. "Unbelievable."

Courtney, meanwhile, let out an incredulous laugh.

"What's the police take on all this?" she asked.

"Detective Rojas said there's only one theory according to her boss, Picado. It's that this Garcia, or whatever his name is, must have belonged to a gang and either squealed on them or threatened to, so they tried to get rid of him. He escaped in the boat, but they tracked him down and attacked him, thinking they had finished him off in the explosion. Then they found out that we had rescued him, so they went to the hospital and took him away before he talked to the police."

"Do they think it was Lobo?"

"They think he's behind this all," Dana said.

"Maybe they stole Tino's birds, and they hurt him. And we walked in and interrupted them before they could take the rest of the birds."

"Mr. Clean with the tattoo head too?" Courtney asked.

"Maybe they were all part of Lobo's gang and Tino was caught in the middle of everything," Dana said.

"They looked like regular old tourists to me, not like any smuggler or poacher I've seen around here," Benny said.

"Well, let's find out," Dana exclaimed.

BACK AT MARIPOSA BEACH, they stopped at the bookstore "slash" cafe. Ringo went inside like he owned the place.

"Who is this adorable furry fella?" Mindy asked.

"It's Tino's dog."

Mindy frowned. "Why do you have that odd bird man's dog?"

"It's a long story. I'll tell you later."

"What are you up to, Nancy Drew?" Mindy asked. Dana rolled her eyes at the Nancy Drew comment, then gave her the CliffsNotes on what had been going on.

"Oh, my word. Please tell me you're going to stop sticking your nose into this?"

"Don't ask questions you don't want answers for."

She asked Amalfi about the birdwatchers. Amalfi had overheard they were staying at an Airbnb nearby, but they didn't mention its location.

Dana scrunched her mouth at the bad news. Then her face lit up. "Big Mike rented them ATVs and other equipment. And he requires a local address."

DANA, Courtney, and Benny headed next door to Big Mike's Surf Shop.

"Whoa, you all look like you're on a mission," Big Mike said, smiling as he looked up from the counter at the trio entering his shop.

Dana asked about the birdwatchers. Big Mike confirmed they'd rented four ATVs to go off-roading in the mountains. They returned a few hours later. "Everything was on the up and up," he said.

"So, you have their local address?" Dana asked.

"Sure do," Big Mike said. "You want me to violate my surf shop owner-client privilege?"

Dana looked at him askew.

"Just joshing, girl. No big whoop. Hold on a sec."

A few moments later, Dana secured the address.

"I know that place," Benny began, "I managed the closing for Marisol Arias." He paused, skepticism clear in his tone. "I can't imagine her renting to people being involved with Lobo or any of his shady operations. Marisol's good people."

Dana looked thoughtful. "Marisol... the yoga instructor?" Memories of a complicated old case flashed before her eyes.

Marisol and her cousin had been involved in the messy dispute over the Casa Verde property, and it was Dana who had unraveled the mystery behind his subsequent murder. Since then, Dana and Marisol had fostered a deep bond. Marisol had even set up a yoga studio in town. She had purchased a house to rent to tourists looking for short stays. It was a nice extra source of income for her.

"I'll call Marisol to see what's up with these people," Dana said, reaching for her phone.

CHAPTER FOURTEEN

As the trio left Big Mike's Surf Shop on Ark Row, they found themselves on the main street of Mariposa Beach. The street had a pleasant rhythm of its own that Dana liked, with the steady crash of the ocean waves on one side and the formidable backdrop of the mountains on the other. Dana watched folks dancing with the waves and sunbathers lounging on the sandy shores. Guilt came back as she looked at Courtney. They should be out there in the sun and having fun, not being dragged around in a case.

As Benny drove the SUV away from the coast, the road wound its way up the mountain, presenting panoramic views of the beach below and the mountains that seemed to embrace the small town. About a mile up, Benny made a right turn into a posh, gated, residential neighborhood. Large, lavish homes peeked from behind tall privacy walls and meticulously maintained hedges.

Dana's phone buzzed as a call connected. "Marisol," she greeted. As they chatted, Dana asked her about the guests currently renting her property.

Marisol's voice oozed warmth as she spoke about them.

"They're wonderful guests, truly. Have asked for little. And they've settled in for two weeks."

"Are they really just here for birdwatching?" Dana inquired, keeping her voice neutral.

Marisol chuckled softly. "Well, they're not your average bird watchers. They're ornithologists. They're here on some big project, something about the rare species around these parts and how to protect them and get them to make more birds."

Dana told Benny and Courtney about the bird watchers. "Wow, scientist, really?" Courtney said.

"I didn't see that guy with a shaved head with a tattoo as a scientist," Benny added.

"Well, it was a tattoo of a bird," Dana said.

Benny entered the access code given by Marisol into a keypad and, a second later, the gate opened. Benny slowly drove onto the property as the gate automatically closed behind them.

They took in the opulent surroundings. "Quite the luxurious setup for bird nerds," Courtney said.

"They're professionals... ornithologists, Courtney, not nerds," Dana corrected.

"Still, I pictured scientists in rugged tents amidst dense forests, not these posh homes."

Benny chimed in, steering the car towards Marisol's house. "If their work allows them the comfort of a proper bed over roughing it outdoors, why wouldn't they choose this?" He gestured to the elegant home before them. "Besides, rent split among six people makes this place very affordable. These aren't San Francisco rents. Yet," Benny said with a grin.

They parked in front of the house and made their way to the front door. They saw a woman peer out from a window. The front door opened before Dana could ring the doorbell.

The woman was in her early thirties and had cropped black

hair; she stood there looking at them askew. "Who are you?" she asked with a German accent.

Before Dana could reply, her face flashed recognition. "I know you. You own the bookstore. You were up in Tino's Bird Sanctuary."

Dana felt surprised at how much this woman knew about her. "Um, that's right. May we come in?"

The woman stood leaning on the door for a moment as if deciding whether to let them in. After another moment, she stepped aside. "Come in."

She led them into the living room. Another woman joined them from upstairs. Dana recognized her redhead from the security video of her bookstore.

Dana extended introductions for herself, Benny, and Courtney. The two women were being standoffish, but Dana understood she would have her guard way up too if three strangers showed up at her front door unannounced with access to a secured gated community.

But the women seemed to relax. "I'm Ina Esser. This is Kathy Hixson."

"What's all this about?" Kathy said. Hixson sounded American.

Dana apologized for the drop-by and explained what was going on with Tino as Ina and Kathy exchanged nervous glances.

"I'll be honest. We're terrified. That's why we aren't with the others out in the field," Ina said.

Kathy and Ina explained their role in this messy case. They were ornithologists, in Costa Rica to set up a study on Tino's land and in public land that surrounded his place so as to understand why it was such a haven for the scarlet macaws and other parrots.

"Tino has done a wonderful job there on his own for over

twenty years with those birds. All self-taught. And I'd put his skills up with any ornithologist with a doctorate that I know," Ina said.

"He warned us about poachers. It's been a growing problem. It's the biggest threat to these endangered birds," Ina added.

"Then we heard about what happened over there and how the Coast Guard had to intervene. And then Tino disappears. It's scary," Kathy said.

"You think all this happened because of those birds?" Dana asked.

"Well, as soon as Tino vanished, we noticed many of the birds in his aviary had been stolen. So we figured it's all connected," Ina said.

"Seems that way," Dana agreed.

Ina continued: "We were trying to rescue the parrots that were left, and that's when you showed up on that day. But Ivan didn't know it was you until later. He just panicked when he saw you all inside Tino's house. He was scared that you were the poachers, so he ran away."

"Is Ivan the guy with the shaved head and the bird tattoo on the back of his head?" Dana asked.

Ina and Kathy smiled. "That's him. He looks a bit intimidating. But he's a brilliant ornithologist," Ina said.

Kathy added, "His name is Doctor Ivan Legasov with the Russian Society for the Conservation and Study of Birds in Moscow. He was doing a fellowship at the Cornell Lab of Ornithology, which is where Ina and I work."

"There are six of you here?" Dana asked.

"That's right. Besides Ivan and us, there is Dr. Herman Erbel from Germany, Dr. Tony Smith with Cornell, and Dr. Wilmer Rincon, a local ornithologist with the University of Costa Rica. He set this project up since he was friends with Tino, who allowed us unfettered access to his land, 24/7."

"Herman, Tony, Wilmer, and Ivan are over at Tino's place right now, trying to rescue those birds from the dang poachers. We've been here on pins and needles, waiting for news from them. And if need be, to contact the authorities."

"What do you think happened to Tino?" Dana asked.

"It's obvious. The poachers killed him. He died protecting those birds," Ina said.

Kathy nodded. "The illegal bird trade here in Costa Rica is lucrative. Exotic birds, especially the rare ones that you see up by Tino's place, can fetch thousands on the black market."

"You saw Tino getting killed?" Dana asked.

Ina and Kathy shook their heads.

"No. But, it's obvious. He would never leave those birds and his animals alone like that," Ina said.

"We can't find his beloved dog, Ringo."

"He's with us," Dana explained. She told them about not wanting to leave the dog on his own. "He's back at my place, getting the stink eye from my cat."

"Oh, thank goodness; we were worried sick," Kathy said.

"What about the fella that was shot, Garcia? Do you know who he is?" Benny asked.

"No. We're not familiar with him. When we heard there was a boat chase and they shot someone, we figured it was a Lobo gang dispute," Ina said.

"Another thing that had us stumped — how did Ivan vanish into thin air off that cliff when I was chasing him?" Dana asked.

The women smiled. "It sounds like you didn't find the secret pathway?" Ina said with a grin.

"I knew it!" Benny said.

"There's a secret pathway?" Dana said, sounding surprised.

"Where does it go?" Courtney asked.

"Down to the beach. There is a lovely cove down there. Nice and calm. It's where Tino docked his boat," Ina said.

"It goes all the way down there? Three hundred some feet?" Dana was doubtful.

"It's like a tunnel. Not suitable if you're claustrophobic," Ina replied.

"Tino's parents built it when he was young. After he inherited the property, he reinforced it and made it safer. There is a trapdoor at the edge of the cliff that's hidden under tall grass and shrubbery. Hard to find it if you don't know it's there."

"That explains Ivan's disappearing act. I was right in that area, and I didn't see a trap door," Benny said. "And I was looking for an entrance."

"That's why Tino kept it hidden, to avoid trespassers," Ina said.

"Maybe Lobo found it. And that's why Tino is missing," Dana said.

"I'm afraid that's a possibility," Ina said.

"Hold on. You said Tino has a boat down there?" Dana asked.

"Yes, but it's missing, too. At first we thought Tino took it out somewhere. But when we heard about the explosion, we worried it was his boat, and he was the man shot. Not this Garcia person," Kathy said.

This case just kept getting stranger by the minute. Was Garcia on Tino's boat? Why was he chasing Lobo? And what did they do with poor Tino? Those thoughts angered Dana.

One way or another. I'm going to get to the bottom of this mess.

CHAPTER FIFTEEN

Back inside of Benny's SUV, the three sat in contemplative silence, digesting their latest findings.

Courtney broke the silence. "Hold on — so these supposed shady birdwatchers were actually collaborating with Tino to save the birds?"

"Exactly. I was way wrong about them. We've got bona fide bird specialists in the mix. Helping Tino. I was certain they were on Lobo's side," Dana said.

Benny chuckled. "Yeah, especially that Ivan fellow. Shaved head, intimidating tattoo, and then bolting when he saw us at Tino's place. He doesn't fit the typical bird scientist mold."

"Lesson of the day: Looks can be deceiving," Dana said.

Courtney leaned forward, urgency in her voice. "So, what's our next move?"

"We need to go back to Tino's place. I want a closer look at that hidden pathway and the cove," Dana said.

Benny was already turning the ignition. "Got it."

"Hold on," Dana interjected. "Let's not drive there. Taking a boat will be quicker."

"How are we going to scale that enormous cliff leading to Tino's house?"

Dana's eyes sparkled with excitement. "Ina mentioned the secret pathway. It descends right from Tino's estate to the secluded beach below and then to a cove which is linked to the inlet. If Tino moored his boat there, that means a boat can go in. So if Ivan took the pathway down, we can take it up. All we need is someone with a boat to give us a ride."

Courtney and Benny exchanged impressed glances. "So, that's how those boats seemed to appear out of thin air that day," Courtney mused.

"Bingo," Dana confirmed. "I wish we had investigated it when we were at the beach with Garcia. But with him nearly dying and the subsequent chaos, I didn't think to explore the inlet and cove."

Courtney grimaced. "I'm not eager to hop on those jet skis again."

"We'll hitch a ride on a proper boat this time," Dana said with a grin.

With a renewed sense of purpose, Benny steered the SUV back towards Mariposa Beach.

AT THE HEART of Mariposa Beach sat two popular boat rental establishments: one owned by Bill Kingman, a Floridian expat with a gleaming catamaran for the tourists, and the other by Captain Geronimo Diaz, a seasoned mariner whose lineage traced back to over a century of local fishermen.

The days of fishing were long behind Captain Geronimo. Now he ferried eager tourists out for deep-sea adventures. He was also the unofficial pier master of Pier 1. Dana didn't know why it was called that, since it was the only one in Mariposa Beach. "Only Pier" seemed more appropriate.

"As we're in peak tourist season, they both might be fully booked," Benny warned.

"We have a backup. We drive to Tino's place and then descend to the beach," Dana suggested.

Ever the optimist, Benny added, "It's a Monday morning, though. Odds might favor us."

They spotted Captain Geronimo aboard his vessel. Dana rushed out of the SUV to approach him before he set sail. She quickly briefed him about their urgent need to reach Morpho Bay.

Adjusting the sports visor cap that proudly declared him CAPTAIN and showcased the logo for his business — a morpho butterfly resting on an anchor — Captain Geronimo stroked his gray stubble in thought. "Well, that's quite the tale," he mused, glancing at his wristwatch. "Had a noon slot open up because of a cancellation, and I'm free till three. Hop on."

As Dana, Benny, and Courtney stepped onto Captain Geronimo's boat, they were struck by the meticulously organized deck. The coils of ropes were arranged in perfect circles, the polished wood reflected the morning sun, and the faint scent of salt and fish lingered in the air.

"Hold on to the side rails, especially as we head out of the bay and it gets choppy until we hit the open water," Captain Geronimo advised as he deftly began undocking. His hands danced on the controls, moving with an ease that spoke of years spent on these waters.

The boat's engine hummed to life, and within moments they were cruising through the tranquil waters of Mariposa Bay. It was a lovely morning, but the group's tense demeanor was a contrast to the serene backdrop. Each was lost in different thoughts about the mission ahead.

As they approached the mouth of the bay, the water grew choppier, just as the captain had warned. The boat swayed more aggressively, every wave causing it to rise and fall in rhythm. Courtney gripped the side of the boat, her knuckles white, while Benny kept a watchful eye on the horizon to avoid sea-motion sickness.

Breaking the tension, a welcome sight appeared on the starboard side. A group of dolphins playfully jumped in and out of the water, their slick bodies glistening. They seemed to be grinning at them. Their joyful acrobatics kept pace with the boat, and for a moment the trio smiled, not thinking about Lobo as they took in the incredible display on the water.

Dana pointed towards the small beach ahead. "There it is," she whispered, as Tino's house came into view. Perched high on the cliff, it stood as a lone sentinel overlooking the vast expanse of the ocean and the beach below. The house seemed ominous with everything that was going on.

"Hold on tight. We're going into Morpho Bay," Captain Geronimo said. His experienced eyes scanned the area as he gently decreased the throttle, slowing the boat. The bay, known for its clear blue waters and secluded nature, was calm today—only the faintest of ripples disturbed its surface.

With precision, he steered the vessel toward the inlet, a narrow passage flanked by tall, moss-covered rocks on either side. The boat glided smoothly through the inlet, where the high cliffs created a serene, almost eerie quiet. The inlet broadened as they moved further in, the water shimmering in various shades of turquoise and deep blue.

As they approached a sheltered spot, Captain Geronimo dropped the boat's anchor. "This is a good spot. We're shielded from any prying eyes, and the water is shallow enough for you to disembark. And we can leave from here in a hurry, if need be," he announced, lowering a sturdy stepladder over the boat's side.

One by one, Dana, Benny, and Courtney carefully descended, the cool water reaching their calves. The fine sandy bed underfoot provided a solid grip as they waded their way to the beach.

Turning to the boat, Dana shouted, "Thanks, Captain! How long can you wait?"

"Don't you worry about me," Captain Geronimo responded with a grin, adjusting his sports visor. "I'll anchor out in the bay, keeping an eye on the boat and any smugglers who might wander our way. Just give me a shout or wave when you're ready to head back. If I see something dangerous heading our way, I'll blow my horn three times."

With that assurance, the trio made their way towards the beach. The looming cliffs seemed like a presage of the challenges that awaited them.

CHAPTER SIXTEEN

THE COVE WAS A SLICE OF SERENITY, NESTLED BETWEEN high rock walls and blanketed with fine golden sand. The gentle lapping of the waves created a soothing melody that harmonized with the distant cries of seagulls. You could see the long, slender shadows of palm trees stretched out as the day progressed.

The trio moved further in amidst a mesmerizing dance of lights created by the reflection of the sun on the water. The craggy faces of the cliffs around them bore testament to an ancient and unending battle against the elements. At the base of these cliffs, where the waves and rock met, were the entrances to several sea caves. Their openings looked like dark voids, contrasting with the brighter shades of the cove.

Feeling a mixture of trepidation and excitement, Dana led the group towards the largest of the sea caves. The air inside was damp, and the echo of their footsteps suggested the cave stretched deeper than it had first appeared.

Dana's flashlight beam landed on something that looked out of place in the natural surroundings of the cave: a sturdy mooring post rising from the ground, carved intricately from beach wood. It was a masterpiece of craftsmanship, with delicate grooves and patterns detailing the natural grains and knots in the wood. The rich deep-brown color of the post was a stark contrast to the gray, damp walls of the cave. At its base, signs of wear showed where ropes had been repeatedly tied and untied, suggesting its frequent use for a boat.

"Look at this," she whispered, reaching out to trace the etchings with her finger. "This has Tino's touch all over it."

Benny, approaching, nodded in agreement. "He always had a knack for making functional things beautiful. Similar to the wooden gate on Tino's property. This is definitely his style."

"This has to be it," Dana whispered excitedly. "Tino's boat must have been right here, hidden away from anyone's view, and then that pathway..." Her voice trailed off as she looked deeper into the cave, eager to find where it led.

Dana cursed herself for not bringing a flashlight, but she used her cell phone's flashlight app, as did Courtney and Benny. Beams of light, however inadequate, sliced through the dimness of the cave.

As Dana, Benny, and Courtney ventured deeper into the cave, they marveled at its vastness. From the beach, the entrance had appeared as a narrow slit in the rocks, but inside the cavern expanded in unexpected directions, its grandeur hidden behind the modest facade. Stalactites dripped from the ceiling, shimmering like icicles. The walls of the cave, damp and glistening, echoed the muted, rhythmic lapping of the water outside. Pools of seawater, trapped during high tide, reflected fleeting glimmers of their flashlight beams, making the cave seem like a world scattered with stars.

Dana kept thinking about the hundreds of thousands of years it took to create this cavern. *Amazing.*

Her beam caught a glint on the ground, and she froze, her eyes narrowing. "Over there." She directed the light to a metal cage, its door ajar. Inside, brilliant feathers of red, yellow, and blue fluttered, their hues reflected on the cave walls. The beauty of the scene stood in stark contrast to the desolation of the cave.

"Scarlet macaws," Benny said, looking around at the aftermath of the smuggler's foul deeds.

The very sight of the cage, juxtaposed against the natural beauty of the cave, made Dana's blood run cold. "Those monsters," she murmured, rage and determination clear in her voice. "They must've discovered the secret pathway and used it as a covert route, bringing the stolen birds from the cliff top right down here and onto their boat. Maybe that's why Garcia was chasing them. He's not with Lobo, but he, too, was helping save the birds."

"But the ornithologists didn't know who he was. It's six in their group, not seven," Benny said.

"So who the heck was this Garcia person? Friend or foe?" Dana wondered. "And where did they take him when they kidnapped him from the hospital?"

"And Tino. If he's alive," Benny said. "It has to be Lobo. But kidnapping, shooting Garcia, it seems a lot to risk for these birds."

"Dr. Esser said they had already stolen six figures in street value. That's not chicken feed," Dana said. "Let's try to find the secret pathway."

They searched until the horn from Captain Geronimo's boat thundered three long times.

"That can't be good," Courtney said.

The trio ran out of the cave back onto the beach. Captain Geronimo had navigated the boat closer. He put a bullhorn to his mouth: "There is a boat heading this way, fast. Through the binoculars I saw three angry looking men. We better leave. They'll be here in less than ten minutes."

"That has to be Lobo!" Dana said.

"Let's not stick around to find out," Courtney said as she ran into the water.

Dana and Benny followed suit. Captain Geronimo maneuvered the boat perfectly, so all they had to do was reach out to the ladder and climb aboard. Once all three were safely inside the boat, the engine roared to life as Captain Geronimo expertly maneuvered the boat, water spraying in all directions from the inlet out to the open water.

Courtney's voice was pitched high, edged with fear. "I see them!" The boat abruptly changed course, heading toward them. "He's chasing us!"

But the captain didn't seem fazed. "That old rust bucket? It doesn't stand a chance against my beauty here." Yet his tense grip on the wheel told another story.

Suddenly, two echoing gunshots rang out across the water, making everyone duck.

"They're shooting!" Benny cried out, hastily bringing out the binoculars to get a clearer view. "Wait, they're just firing into the air."

A garbled voice emerged, amplified by a PA speaker. "Don't return! This is private land. Cross us and you won't live to tell the tale!"

Dana's heart raced as she watched the boat make a sharp turn, mercifully retreating towards the cove. Courtney's face was pale, her hands shaking visibly. "That was too close," she said.

The boat's engine hummed, its intensity matching the tension on board. They were hurtling back to Mariposa Beach at a speed Dana hadn't previously experienced on Captain Geronimo's boat. Lobo might not be chasing them anymore, but the captain wasn't taking any chances.

Breaking the heavy silence, Dana glanced gratefully at the captain: "Thank you, Captain. You saved us."

A fleeting smile was on the captain's usually stony face. "Just doing what's right."

As the familiar silhouette of Mariposa Beach's pier came into view, Dana's sense of urgency returned. The mystery of Tino, Garcia, and the birds weighed heavily on her, and she knew the danger was far from over because she would not stop her investigation.

CHAPTER SEVENTEEN

DANA, BENNY, AND COURTNEY TRIED TO CALM THEIR racing hearts after the harrowing escape from Lobo. Dana paced restlessly on Pier 1, frustration evident in each step. "Every single time I try to investigate Tino's place, I'm literally chased away."

Courtney leaned against a nearby palm, her face drawn. "Maybe the universe is screaming at us to back off."

"We should hand this over to the cops," Benny said. "This is way beyond our depth."

Dana dialed Detective Rojas. After detailing their latest run-in, she pressed, "Any leads on Tino or this Garcia person?"

Rojas sighed on the other end. "Tino isn't our top priority right now."

"Lobo could've harmed him, or worse! How is that not urgent?"

"He's an adult," Rojas replied coolly. "And he's only been missing a few days. Maybe he took a spontaneous trip."

Dana didn't believe that for a minute. And she was certain that neither did Rojas, but the powers that be, her superiors like Picado, had other ideas.

"And Garcia? He was abducted, after all."

"Evidence doesn't confirm that. We only know they helped him into a car. Could've been friends."

"Helped? You said he was forcibly shoved into a black SUV."

"That's not how things are looking now."

"After being shot? You can't seriously believe that," Dana snapped.

Rojas's tone turned defensive. "We have to consider every angle. However, we are looking for him. His abrupt exit from the hospital, the gunshot, the boat explosion, and that fake name."

Dana perked up. "So you know who he is?"

Rojas paused for a moment. "We took his fingerprints at the hospital. Just got a match. His real name is Rigoberto Espada."

Dana's heart skipped a beat. "Espada? As in Tino Espada?"

"Yes," Rojas confirmed. "He's Tino's brother."

Dana was reeling. They were brothers. "Why didn't he tell us that? And why the fake name?"

"Those are questions I plan to ask him myself when we find him," Rojas said.

"So two brothers vanish. That's still not urgent?"

"Maybe they went to have fun in Vegas for the week. There is not enough here to pull out all the stops to find the Espada brothers. Sorry, Dana."

Dana sat on the pier. The glow of the sun cast a golden hue over her features. She felt defeated.

Courtney, noticing Dana's intense expression, exchanged a glance with Benny before asking, "What did Detective Rojas say?"

"You won't believe this."

Benny leaned in, intrigued. "Try us."

"First off," Dana began, her tone measured, "Garcia isn't who he claimed to be."

"What do you mean?" Courtney asked.

Dana let the anticipation build for a moment. "His real name is Rigoberto Espada."

Benny's eyes widened in recognition, while Courtney gasped. "Espada? As in...?"

"Exactly. Tino Espada. They're brothers."

The impact caused by the information seemed to hang in the air. The gentle whisper of the ocean waves in the distance provided a stark contrast to the trio's stunned silence.

"That... changes everything," Benny murmured.

"The police don't seem to agree," Dana said.

Courtney frowned, thinking aloud, "So, if they're brothers, maybe Rigoberto was trying to help Tino or vice versa."

"Tino was known for being a hermit. Living alone up there. I'm surprised he has a brother," Benny said.

"Well, everyone has family," Dana said.

Benny shook his head in disbelief. "Two brothers, both in some serious trouble."

"We have to get to the bottom of this," Dana added.

"Um, let's focus on what Benny said. Two brothers, one shot, both missing. They're probably at the bottom of the Pacific. I think we've gone as far as we can," Courtney said, sounding fearful.

"You can be our point of contact and look out in town, since we can't get a reception out there," Dana said.

"So you're going back out there to Tino's place?" Courtney asked.

"It's the only way to figure out what's going on."

"Oh, brother. What are you planning to do?"

"Well, it seems like getting through Tino's cove is where the trouble always starts. I'm wondering if they don't have it under surveillance somehow," Dana said.

"So we go from the top through Tino's house," Benny said.

"That's what I was thinking," Dana said. "Court, you stay here in town, being our eyes and ears. You can let us know if something is happening."

"Nice try, Dana. You have no cell service over there. Even if something happens, I won't be able to get a hold of you. I appreciate you wanting me to stay here for safety, but I'm a big girl. Sure, I'm terrified of Lobo, but I'm going with you!"

Dana smiled. She didn't want Courtney coming along if she was too scared and offered her an excuse for her friend to stay by making it seem like she would help them, but Courtney saw right through her.

"Hold on there," Captain Geronimo's gruff voice boomed behind Dana. The trio had been discussing their plans on the pier by Captain Geronimo's boat, so he'd overheard the entire discussion.

Dana turned to look as the sun's rays deepened the furrows on the captain's weathered skin. His steely eyes locked onto Dana's, a hint of determination shimmering within them. The captain approached them with purpose as he held up a pair of yellow Motorola two-way radios. "Take this," he said, handing her one of the radios. "They are waterproof, have over twenty channels, and their signal strength is unmatched on these waters." He handed the other radio to Courtney. "I'll take Miss Lowe aboard with me. From my boat's tower, she can scout the open water. I'll ensure we're primed for any action that might come our way. If things get too heated, we'll relay a message via the radio, and you can make a quick exit. We'll be there to pick you up."

Dana was taken aback. "Captain, we can't ask for more from

you. You've already done so much, pulling us away from Lobo's grasp. I don't want to put you and your boat in danger."

Captain Geronimo's jaw tightened, and he squared his shoulders. "Lobo has the audacity to threaten me at sea? My family has thrived in these waters here since the 1800s. He might be the terror of many, but out here, I am the force to reckon with. The ocean has molded me, tested my mettle. Given me my livelihood. I'm not letting anyone scare me off." There was a hint of a smirk tugging at the corner of his mouth. "And, Doña Dana, you're part of our fold now. No one, and I mean no one, dares to harm a Mariposa Beach local on my watch."

Tears brimmed in Dana's eyes, and she closed the gap between them, embracing the rugged captain. His tough exterior hid a heart of gold. But she knew their mission wasn't over; it was just beginning.

CHAPTER EIGHTEEN

BENNY WAS BEHIND THE WHEEL OF HIS LAND CRUISER AS they drove to Tino's place. Captain Geronimo and Courtney headed out that way via the boat. Dana made two calls before her signal died. First she called the ornithologists and spoke with Dr. Ina Esser. She wanted the exact details of the secret pathway. Ina handed the phone to Dr. Ivan, who had taken that route dozens of times. Ivan spoke with the Russian accent that Amalfi had picked up when he visited the bookstore.

Ivan gave her detailed instructions of where to find the entrance. It was located a few feet from the house, toward the edge of the cliff and hidden by shrubbery. "You'll see a piece of rope on the ground that seems out of place. Pull on that, and it will open a wooden hatch that has grass attached to it, so it blends in when closed."

Dana thanked him.

"We'll join you up there since we know the area well now, and if you find those birds, you'll need our help to ensure they're safe or if they needed medical care," Ivan said.

"The more help we can get, the better," Benny said when Dana hung up and informed them.

Dana made her second call. The phone line crackled to life as she patched in with Detective Rojas. To her surprise, the brusquer voice of the senior detective, Jorge Picado, echoed in the background.

"I've put you on speakerphone so Detective Picado can be updated too," Rojas explained.

With a steadying breath, Dana recounted their nerve-racking encounter with Lobo and shared their plan to rendezvous with the ornithologists at Tino's.

"Hold it right there," Picado interjected sharply. "You're not stepping foot on that property. It's part of an ongoing investigation."

Dana felt her anger bubbling. "I was told Tino's disappearance wasn't being treated as a crime. That the Espada brothers are in Vegas. Which is it, Detective? A crime scene or two adults on vacation?"

Picado seemed momentarily flustered. "You can't just saunter onto private property."

"Actually," Benny said smoothly, "the ornithologists have prior written consent from Tino to be on his land. So, technically, we won't be trespassing."

"We're investigating the Rigoberto Espada shooting, and the last thing we need is civilians messing things up," Picado said, without bothering to hide his irritation.

Dana retorted, "I didn't even see police tape at Tino's property or any signs of the police or forensic investigators. Doesn't look like a crime scene to me."

The silence from the other end was palpable. "You know where we'll be, Detective," Dana said, hanging up.

UPON REACHING TINO'S PLACE, a strange sense of familiarity washed over Dana. The surroundings seemed frozen from the moment she had journeyed through the woods to this secluded spot, led by the enigmatic Tino. She hoped he was okay, fearing the worst.

Benny paused before entering the property, scanning the area with sharp eyes. "Everything appears clear," he murmured, though the slight edge in his voice betrayed his wariness.

Suddenly, the radio's static pierced the quiet, causing both Dana and Benny to jump. After a shared sheepish chuckle over their nervous reaction, Courtney's voice chimed in. "We're positioned off the cove. All's calm here."

"Copy that, Courtney. We've arrived on our end, and it's silent too." Dana met Benny's gaze, feeling the weight of the situation. "Let's move."

Nodding in agreement, Benny eased the vehicle forward and entered Tino's property.

Tino's carport still sat empty, filling Dana with dread. It was now three days since his disappearance. But to her surprise, there were two ATVs parked in front of the house.

The ornithologist with a bird tattoo on the side of his shaved head was there, watching them pull in.

It was the same man Dana had seen on Tino's property, but this time he didn't run. He smiled and waved. Dana was relieved to see Dr. Ivan there and not one of Lobo's armed thugs. Next to him was Dr. Ina Esser.

"Dana Kirkpatrick and Benny Campos, I presume," Ivan said with a smile.

"You got up here fast," Benny said.

"We can climb right up the hill with this bad boy," Ivan said, pointing to the ATV.

Dana shook his hand. "Nice to meet you. Last time I saw

you, you vanished over the cliff like magic," she said with a smile.

"Sorry about that," he said, wiping the sweat from his brow. "I've had run-ins with poachers in Brazil, West Africa, faced pirates in the Gulf of Aden, narrowly escaped bandits in Belize, and FARC rebels in the Colombian jungle, so I've learned that at the first sign of trouble I don't hang around. I run."

"Understood, especially since it seems this poacher and smuggler Lobo has been muscling into Tino's land," Dana said.

Ivan nodded solemnly. He gestured for them to sit on a couple of makeshift stools on the front porch.

"Tino made these from driftwood he collects from the beach below," Ina said as they sat down.

"The mooring post below is exquisite. I assume that's Tino's craftsmanship as well?" Benny asked.

"The man is skilled," Ivan said. "He has quite the woodsman workshop in that shed back there."

"I didn't realize he had such talents," Benny said. "I just knew him as the reclusive birdman living up here in the middle of nowhere." There was a tinge of guilt in Benny's voice. But Tino had the reputation of an eccentric recluse, happier spending time with birds than people.

"Tino and us, we've been collaborating for a while now," Ivan began, his tone serious yet tinged with admiration. "Scarlet macaws, magnificent creatures that they are, have been increasingly targeted for the illegal pet trade. Their bright plumage and intelligence make them a prized catch. And Tino, he's been instrumental in their conservation. His property is one of the few sanctuaries where these birds can safely breed and thrive."

Dana leaned in, intrigued. "So, how does Lobo fit into all this?"

Ivan's face darkened, a mixture of anger and fear clouding his eyes. "Lobo is... a menace. Not just a petty smuggler. He's practically a kingpin in the illegal wildlife trade. From what we've gathered, he's been after Tino for a while. They have history."

Benny interjected, "We've had our own run-ins with him. He seems to be searching for something specific. He already stole the birds in Tino's aviary, yet he's still hanging around here. Any idea why?"

"Lobo believes Tino knows the location of a secret nesting site — a veritable gold mine for someone in his line of business. Capture one macaw from a normal habitat, and you've got a good haul. But find the nesting site, and you've got generations of birds to exploit. The macaw nesting season lasts from January through April, so we're right at the start of it. Which is why Lobo has been so aggressive lately. But Tino has been fortified up here on the cliff. There is only one way off the road you took. He can watch the winding road from here as well as the open water. So he knows when they're coming with plenty of time to batten down the hatches to protect the birds and himself. But somehow Lobo must have gotten to him."

Dana's eyes widened in realization. "So, you think Lobo might have taken Tino to force the location out of him?"

"It's a plausible theory. From what we know of Lobo, he'll stop at nothing to get what he wants. And if he found out about that secret pathway, he could sneak up here and surprise Tino," Ivan said.

"You think that's what happened?" Dana asked.

"Lobo got the drop on Tino, and that's the only way I can see him doing that."

"Did you meet Tino's brother, Rigoberto Espada? Goes by Beto," Dana asked.

Ivan shook his head. "He didn't talk about his family or his past. He's a very secretive, private person. Is his brother mixed up in this somehow?"

"You could say that. He's the man who was chasing Lobo's boat. Lobo shot him and blew up his boat. Me and Courtney happened to be out here on jet skis, and we were able to rescue him. But he, too, is now missing. That's Tino's brother."

"This case gets weirder by the minute," Ina said.

"And Tino? Do you think he'd give in?" Benny asked.

Ivan let out a slow breath, choosing his words carefully. "Tino dedicated his life to these birds. He'd do anything to protect them. But facing a man like Lobo, that's a different challenge."

Processing the weight of the situation, Dana rubbed her temples. "We need to find Tino before Lobo goes to any extreme."

"And we'll help," Ivan said. "Tino's not just a collaborator; he's a friend. Lobo might have his goons, but we have knowledge, expertise, and the will to save our feathery friends and their protector. I just hope we're not too late."

———————

CHAPTER NINETEEN

THERE WAS URGENCY IN IVAN'S EYES AS HE MENTIONED THE secluded nesting spot Tino had protected so fiercely. "After months of building trust, Tino finally revealed the location to us, right before he vanished. My team is now hiking up there to ensure it's secure," Ivan said, holding up his portable radio. "If Lobo has discovered its whereabouts, we'll get an update."

"On the waterfront, we have our own eyes and ears. Captain Geronimo and Courtney are stationed on a boat just off the cove. If Lobo or any of his men approach from that side, we'll be the first to know," Dana replied, raising her own radio in solidarity.

The shared determination in their eyes promised a united front against any impending threat. Tino might be dead, Dana thought, but she was going to do all she could to protect his beloved parrots from these smugglers' grubby hands.

Benny glanced around, visibly concerned. "What's our next move?"

"Lobo's thefts from the aviary didn't end up here," Ivan began, his gaze on the horizon. "We're convinced he used the secret pathway to transport them to a boat waiting in the sea cave beneath the cove."

Dana remembered their previous findings. "We saw evidence of their captivity — the empty cages and scattered feathers near the mooring posts."

"Given the intricate network of caves down there, it's likely Lobo has hidden the birds in one of them. He might be planning to locate the nesting spot before he smuggles all the birds out," Ivan said.

"While your team keeps watch over the nesting area, I think we should head to the cove and explore those caves," Dana said.

Ina opened a duffel bag to reveal an array of equipment. She pulled out two heavy-duty flashlights and handed them over. "These are state-of-the-art lantern flashlights, boasting 30,000 lumens. Waterproof and fully charged. They should serve you well in those murky caves," she said.

"Much better than my cellphone flashlight, thank you," Dana said.

Ivan led Dana and Benny towards the cliff's edge, to the very spot where he had mysteriously disappeared during their previous encounter. The breeze was crisp, carrying with it the briny scent of the sea. Dana looked around, trying to spot any signs of the secret entrance that had eluded her before.

Stopping near a withered tree trunk that seemed long dead and forgotten, Ivan bent down. To a casual observer, it looked like he was merely inspecting the ground. But then he reached into the hollow of the dead trunk and pulled out a thick, rugged rope hidden inside.

With a quick, practiced motion, Ivan tugged sharply on the rope. A section of the ground beside the tree, previously indistinguishable from the duff and underbrush, peeled back like a curtain, revealing a hatch door.

Dana's eyes widened in surprise. "Incredible! It's perfectly camouflaged."

Benny crouched down to inspect the hatch, touching the edges, marveling at the craftsmanship. "This is no ordinary pathway. They designed this with great care to remain hidden."

Ivan nodded, his expression serious. "It's been here for generations. The locals say it was initially a smuggler's route during colonial times. Tino's family stopped using it. But Tino began working to restore it, and he made it safer. He shored it up. Built this hidden hatch door in the ground. And he kept it a secret until he showed me when we first started collaborating."

"All right then, lead the way," Dana said. "Let's see what's down there."

The Russian carefully opened the hatch door all the way, and the faint sound of echoing waves crashing against the rocks wafted up from the depths, beckoning them onwards. One by one, they began their descent into the secret pathway; the door shut quietly behind them, once again concealing its existence from the world above.

Dana paused at the entrance, her pulse quickening as she allowed the beam of her flashlight to explore the darkness within. The tunnel opened like a gaping mouth of shadows, immediately plunging sharply downward in a forewarning of the steep journey ahead. Its walls glistened with moisture, and every so often droplets journeyed down their rugged surface to the ground. The earthy scent of moss, combined with the tang of the sea, filled her senses.

"Use the rope if you need extra support. It's anchored to that metal hitch in the rock," Ivan directed, showing the fixture with his flashlight. A sturdy rope lay sprawled across the ground, its length bridging the gap from the top of the entrance all the way to the cove below. A makeshift handrail.

Taking a deep breath, she stepped in, her rubber-soled shoes making soft, squishing noises on the slightly wet pathway. The tunnel was narrow; in some parts, she felt the cold, rough walls pressing against her shoulders, forcing her to move sideways. The ceiling overhead was uneven — sometimes she could stand to her full height, while in other parts she had to duck to avoid jagged outcroppings.

Ivan led the way, moving through the route with an agility and assurance that came from familiarity. Behind Dana, Benny occasionally offered a word of encouragement when the path became treacherous.

The descent was unrelenting. With each step, Dana felt the weight of the earth pressing on her, and the air grew colder, thicker. The path would twist so tightly she lost sight of Ivan up ahead, relying solely on the glow of his flashlight to guide her.

As they went deeper, the sounds of the outside forest world grew distant, replaced by the haunting whisper of the sea. The echo of dripping water resonated, and a rhythmic pounding suggested they were nearing the waves crashing into the cove.

The steepness of the pathway was such that, at times, Dana felt she was going down a scary, wobbly ladder instead of walking. She imagined this secret path had seen its share of scraped knees and elbows and even worse. Several times she lost her footing on a slippery rock but was quickly steadied by Benny's firm grip.

Finally, after what felt like hours but was likely mere minutes, the pathway leveled out. Dana could feel the air change again; it was moist with a salty tang. The echo of waves grew louder, and so did the cry of seagulls. And she could see the sunlight.

The beam of her flashlight revealed the end of the tunnel, opening out into one of the sea caves. The water reflected the intermittent light, shimmering and dancing on the cave walls. They had arrived at the cove.

Catching her breath, Dana looked around, the enormity of their journey sinking in. "Incredible," she whispered, the word echoing softly back to her. "Tino truly had a treasure of a secret here."

"One that a smuggler like Lobo would covet," Benny said ominously.

CHAPTER TWENTY

In her days as a journalist, Dana had profiled a renowned cave explorer in the Bay Area. That assignment had led her on a spelunking adventure at Point Reyes's Limantour Beach. For a novice at hiking caves like her, it was both a thrilling and daunting experience. That was more than a decade ago. Since then, her only subterranean escapade had been a few visits to the Sutro Baths Cave in San Francisco. Yet, none of those experiences had prepared her for the grandeur unfolding before her.

The vast interior of the cave was accentuated by the soft, dark sand that stretched to meet the water's edge. Anchored in this sand were Tino's mooring posts, which would discreetly hide his boat from anyone on the beach or the open water. A clever choice by Tino, Dana thought.

Yet, from this concealed position, one could easily unhook the boat and sail through the tranquil waters of the cave, merging into the cove, and eventually into the sea beyond. These were the very posts that Dana and Courtney had stumbled upon earlier before Captain Geronimo's urgent horn blast had warned them of Lobo's approach. The empty space now echoed with the absence of the bird cage she had spotted there.

The evidence was mounting: Lobo had infiltrated Tino's secret boat cave and the concealed path leading to his place.

A flicker of hope that she would spot Tino's boat securely anchored surged in Dana. But the boat was nowhere to be seen. "Where could you be?" she silently wondered.

With unwavering determination, Ivan, accompanied closely by Ina, spearheaded their exploration. Dana and Benny trailed them closely, leaving the shadow of the cave for the open sands of the cove's beach.

On the beach, Dana's eyes were immediately drawn to Captain Geronimo's vessel. The familiar silhouette of Courtney was visible, waving exuberantly. Almost simultaneously, the radio buzzed, and Courtney's voice filled the air.

"You're safe! Oh, what a relief!" she said with a mix of relief and joy.

Dana pressed the radio close to her mouth, replying, "Thanks, Court. Once this mess is sorted, you'll have to come down here to these caves. It's breathtaking."

Courtney's chuckle came through. "I'm holding you to that, but only once we've put Lobo and this drama behind us."

She continued, "Looks like you've got some company there."

"Indeed. Ivan and Ina have been our guiding lights through all this," Dana said, nodding at the two ornithologists.

"Stay on guard. I'll be watching for Lobo from here," Courtney insisted.

"Appreciate it," Dana replied, switching her focus back to Ivan, who seemed eager to share something.

"Over yonder," Ivan pointed towards the south, "is a cave I've been meaning to explore. According to Tino, there's a waterfall inside. Local maps suggest it's the place where pirates from Robert Louis Stevenson tales would hide their treasures. My hunch is Lobo might hide the parrots there."

Dana's eyes lit up with anticipation. "Then let's not waste time," she declared.

The group, led by Ivan, started the trek towards the mysterious cave.

As Dana, Benny, Ivan, and Ina neared the cave, the brilliant flash of red and blue overhead caught their attention. A majestic scarlet macaw soared gracefully, drawing everyone's eyes upward.

"Wow, just look at that," Dana said, pointing at the beautiful bird.

Ivan watched the bird with a practiced eye. "It's quite rare for macaws to fly this close to the beach. They usually keep to the trees to avoid any territorial conflicts with the gulls," he noted.

Ina smiled. "He's certainly a stunner."

Dana's brow furrowed in curiosity. "How can you tell it's male from this distance?" Dana asked.

"Well, technically, I can't be certain," Ina said. "But male macaws often have broader heads and more robust beaks. Though I'm just making an educated guess here."

Ivan added, "It's odd he's alone, though. Scarlet macaws mate for life and usually move in pairs."

Dana's eyes softened. "That's really touching."

As they drew nearer, the magnificent bird descended, alighting gracefully upon a piece of driftwood near the cave's entrance. Its vibrant plumage stood out starkly against the natural backdrop.

"This is such a rare treat," Ina whispered, a touch of awe in her voice.

Suddenly the parrot began to vocalize, its voice sharp and clear.

"Ayuda, ayuda. Pillos. Pillos. Aquí. Aquí. Ayuda. Ayuda."

Dana blinked in surprise. "I didn't realize macaws could... well, talk."

"Sounds more like he's shouting rather than speaking," Benny said with a laugh.

Ivan and Ina exchanged an amused glance. "Macaws, like most parrots, can mimic a variety of sounds, from human speech to everyday noises," Ivan informed them.

But as if on cue, the macaw began its chant again, its voice urgent: *"Ayuda, ayuda. Pillos. Pillos. Aquí. Aquí. Ayuda. Ayuda."*

Benny's face turned serious. While the others in the group understood varying degrees of Spanish, Benny, as a native speaker, grasped the gravity instantly. "He's saying 'Help, help. Thieves. Thieves. Here. Here. Help. Help.'"

Dana's eyes widened in realization. The group exchanged anxious glances, the weight of the bird's message settling upon them.

"How did they pick that up?" Dana asked.

"Shouting for help, even though he lived out here alone, was probably his way to scare intruders to think there he had his own posse nearby," Ivan said.

"Parrots can only mimic words they hear, so this bird must have learned that from Tino," Ina said.

"Makes sense since the nearest neighbor is several miles down the mountain from Tino's property," Benny said.

"Dare we go in?" Ivan voiced the question that hung in the air.

Dana pondered for a few heartbeats before determination set in. "Let's do it."

Seeing Dana's resolve, the others nodded in agreement.

Quickly, Dana grabbed her radio, contacting Courtney.

"Courtney, we're about to enter another cave, a larger one. Can you keep an eye on us?"

Through the radio, Courtney responded, "Got you in sight with my binoculars."

Dana took a deep breath. "I'll give the squelch button a quick three-click signal every ten minutes. If you don't get that signal, call the authorities immediately. And if I start repeatedly pressing that button, dial them without a second thought."

DANA, Benny, Ivan, and Ina peered inside, gazing in awe at its intimidating size and structure. The facade of the cave was rugged, with moss-covered rocks at the periphery. From where they stood, they could hear the faint sound of water echoing from deep within, hinting at the presence of the majestic water-fall Ivan had spoken about.

"The maps don't do this justice," Ivan whispered, clearly taken aback despite his prior knowledge.

The entrance to their left was a yawning chasm, a vertical drop that seemed to plunge into the bowels of the earth. Its walls were glossy, wet, and reflected the ambient light through a faint shimmer. The occasional droplet of water could be seen descending, catching stray sunrays, creating transient rainbows before merging with the darkness below.

"That's a 140-foot pit," Ina remarked, peering cautiously over the edge. "Rappelling down there would be fun, but I'd suggest we take the walk-in entrance." She gestured to their right.

As they turned to the secondary entrance, Dana noticed the gentle slope leading downwards into the cave's belly. This route was more hospitable, with a narrow pathway flanked by stalag-mites and stalactites, some fusing to form grand pillars.

The deeper they walked, the cooler it became. The ambient light faded, and their flashlights became essential as the path meandered, sometimes broadening into cavernous chambers with awe-inspiring rock formations, and occasionally narrowing, demanding they move in single file.

The group found a massive chamber. A silvery thread of water cascaded from high above, crashing into a crystal-clear pool. The waterfall split scant rays of light, creating prismatic effects across the chamber. The mist it produced gave the entire room a dreamlike quality.

Benny, usually stoic, couldn't help but whistle. "It's like nature's cathedral."

Dana took a step closer to the pool, the cool spray kissing her face. "This... this is otherworldly."

The pool, fed by the waterfall, had a serene aura. The water was transparent, revealing the smooth pebbles and sand on its bed. Tiny fish darted around, their scales catching the light.

Ivan, ever the ornithologist, was scanning the chamber's nooks and crannies. "Birds would love a place like this," he murmured, his eyes searching. "Warm, humid, and away from predators."

Suddenly, Ina, who had ventured further, called, "There's another way out!" She pointed towards the far end of the chamber where the light seemed to peek through another exit, suggesting the cave had a dual entrance.

But the real wonder was the waterfall itself. As they approached, they noticed a passage behind the curtain of water. A secret pathway concealed by the cascade. It was as if the waterfall guarded the cave's most intimate secrets.

Dana, curiosity piqued, mused aloud, "What wonders or secrets might this cave be hiding?"

That's when they heard the screams: *"Ayuda, ayuda. Aquí. Aquí."* Help. Help. Here. Here.

CHAPTER TWENTY-ONE

THE GROUP BEGAN MOVING THEIR FLASHLIGHTS TOWARD the screams.

"Did that bird fly into the cave?" Dana asked, bewildered.

"Doubtful, unless there is another way it can fly in safely," Ivan said.

Then they heard the shouting again: *"Aquí. Aquí!"*

"It's coming from the other side of the waterfall," Ivan said. As they made their way across the cascading water, they stood at the entrance of a larger cavern.

"This cave is so huge it has other caves inside," Benny said.

From this vantage point, they could hear that pleas for help weren't coming from a parrot but a man, who sounded very distraught. They could also hear the squawks of parrots.

"The birds!" Ina said excitedly.

Ivan led the way towards the voice of the man, with Dana and the others following. The flashlights of the four explorers formed a powerful spotlight; they saw several cages full of exotic parrots. And two men lying on the ground, tied up.

Ivan pointed his flashlight at the one man who had been calling for help.

"Tino!" Ivan cried, rushing to his side.

"Oh, thank goodness, it's you," Tino said. The vibrant man who had out-hiked Dana in the woods looked frail after spending days in this dark cave.

Dana joined Ivan, helping Tino as Benny and Ina checked on the other man, who wasn't saying anything, nor was he moving. It was Beto Espada.

"Who did this to you and your brother?" Ivan asked. Dana knew what the answer would be. "Lobo, that no-good rat," Tino said, his voice weak.

The knots binding Tino and Beto were intricately tied, clearly intended to be inescapable. Ivan and Dana wrestled with them, pulling and tugging with all their might, but the ropes held fast, instilling a chill in Dana. "I don't think they were planning to untie him and let him go, ever."

With a swift motion, Ivan drew a hefty knife from a sheath on his leg.

"Going all out, Rambo?" Dana remarked with a grin.

"Never enter the field unprepared," Ivan replied, giving the knife a brief, admiring glance. Without hesitation, he sliced through the ropes securing Tino, each strand parting effortlessly under the blade like it was made of butter.

As Tino's bonds fell away, he groaned, slowly rising to his feet. His wrists bore chafe marks from the tight ropes, and his face was a patchwork of bruises. Despite the obvious abuse he'd suffered, he seemed to be fine.

Ivan handed Tino a water bottle from his pack, which Tino gratefully accepted, gulping down its contents in seconds.

"Any injuries, Tino? Broken bones?" Ivan inquired.

Shaking his head, Tino replied, "No, thankfully," before taking a few steadying breaths. After finishing the water, he added, "But my brother... He's been quiet for the past hour." His voice shook with concern. "Beto, can you hear me?"

Dana's gaze shifted to the figure on the ground, recognizing him as Garcia. He lay there, breaths shallow and strained.

Having freed Beto with a knife as impressive as Ivan's, Ina voiced her concern. "He's alive, but he needs immediate medical attention."

"He hadn't even recovered from his initial wounds when those animals took him!" Tino said.

Rummaging through her backpack, Ina produced a First Aid kit. As she carefully removed Beto's shirt, she commented, "The wound has reopened." She set to work, skillfully dressing it to stabilize him until they could get him to a hospital.

Dana quickly radioed Courtney, updating her on their discovery of Tino and Beto and emphasizing the need for both police and medical assistance. "Consider it done," Courtney assured her through the radio.

Benny glanced around the cavern, a look of concern on his face. "Even if the authorities respond immediately, it might take them a while to reach this secluded spot,"

Tino had moved over to the cages housing his birds. "It'll be all right, my friends. We'll get you out of here and to safety soon," he whispered to them. "Ringo, my poor buddy, has been all alone in the house all this time."

"Ringo is safe. We came back to look for you, saw the house in disarray, so we took Ringo," Dana said with a smile.

"We've been feeding your chickens and goats," Ivan said.

"Thank goodness. Thank you. I've been worried sick about my animals."

Dana was still trying to piece together Lobo's intentions, so she asked Tino, "Why didn't Lobo just take the birds and release you? What's his endgame?"

Tino turned to face the group, a hard expression on his face. "Lobo's appetite for profit knows no bounds. Why be content with just these birds when he can exploit the nesting area on my land? This cove is a haven for turtles to lay their eggs. He covets those eggs as well."

Ivan chimed in, a thoughtful look on his face, "Macaw nesting runs from January to April, while turtle nesting spans from March to November. If Lobo controls both, he'd have a year-long illicit trade of exotic birds and turtle eggs."

"That's what he was after," Tino said. "That beast Lobo was determined to force me into signing a quitclaim deed of my property over to one of his front companies. When I refused, he beat me up. When that didn't work, he abducted my brother Beto from the hospital, to use him as leverage against me, threatening his life and my birds to get what he wanted." Tino's voice was thick with emotion and fury.

Dana's eyes lit up. "Was Beto chasing after Lobo's boat because you were on board?"

Tino gave a somber nod. "Yes. He was staying with me for a few days when Lobo's men ambushed me. They were dragging me onto their boat when Beto, who'd been out walking on the beach, noticed the commotion. We had just reconciled after a long separation and were in the process of rebuilding our brotherly bond. Seeing them take me away in their boat, Beto ran into the cove, commandeered my boat, and gave chase. But Lobo fired at him, making the boat go up in flames. I believed Beto was dead," Tino said, his voice cracking. He took a deep breath and continued sharing his ordeal. "After that, there was chaos on the boat. Lobo's men wanted to abandon their plans. They wanted to get rid of me, a loose end, and then lie low for a while. But Lobo said he was not about to let all this hard work go to waste without his pay day. They spent a few hours at sea until the coast was clear and they went back to the cove where they stashed me. I've been here since then. I mourned Beto's death, so I was shocked, but relieved when a couple days later, they dragged him in here too."

"How awful," Dana said.

Benny shifted anxiously as he looked around. "We need to leave. The last thing we want is Lobo catching us here before the police get here or we'll end up tied up as well, or worse."

"Good idea," Ivan said.

"How do we get him out safely?" Dana looked worriedly at the still-unconscious Beto.

Ivan surveyed the surroundings, then decisively stated, "The terrain towards the beach is relatively even. I can shoulder him and carry him out."

CHAPTER TWENTY-TWO

THE ATMOSPHERE WITHIN THE CAVE WAS STIFLING, EACH breath thick with tension.

Beto lay on the cold cavern floor. His breathing had become even more shallow and strained. The flickering lights from Dana and the team created a ghostly dance of shadows on the cavern walls as they gathered around him.

Ivan kneeled by Beto. He planted his feet firmly and took a moment to gauge the challenge ahead. The cavern's treacherous, uneven floor, wet with patches of moss and pooled water, promised no easy journey.

Crouching low, he slid one arm beneath Beto's knees and the other behind his shoulders. With a grunt, he hoisted the unconscious man, adjusting his grip before expertly transitioning him to his shoulders in a fireman's carry.

Beto wasn't a heavy man — about a buck forty, in his late fifties — but in the precarious environment of the cave, his weight was a test of Ivan's endurance. Every step Ivan took was deliberate, seeking the most stable ground among the rocky hazards. The persistent drip of water from the ceiling and the distant sound of the sea outside were the only noises that accompanied them.

Tino, who had known all the nooks and crannies of the caves on his cove since childhood, led the way. The group's progress was marked by tense silence, punctuated only by an occasional intake of breath or a whispered warning. A few times, Ivan's footing faltered, his boot skidding on a slimy stone or a patch of moss, causing the group to catch their collective breath. But each time Ivan regained his balance, shifted Beto's weight, and pressed forward.

The cave's exit had seemed an eternity away, but as the hint of daylight began to pierce the darkness, their spirits lifted. It was the proverbial light at the end of a tunnel. Dana and Ina were close on Ivan's heels, torches aloft, while Benny scouted ahead, pointing out potential pitfalls.

Closer to the cave's exit, the suspense was nearly tangible. The roar of the surf grew deafening, a reminder of both potential dangers and the promise of safety beyond. The light at the cavern's end beckoned, but the perilous path they'd traversed was a testament to the challenges they still faced.

Finally, with a surge of effort, Ivan emerged into the sunlight with Beto still firmly on his shoulders. The team, one by one, left the oppressive dark of the cave, having navigated its dangers together. Their eyes narrowed against the sudden brightness, struggling to adapt after the gloom of the cave. Tino, imprisoned in the cave's shadows for three days, took the longest to adapt. Tears formed, provoked by the sting of sunlight and the overwhelming relief of once again feeling the open air.

The static from Dana's radio buzzed before Courtney's voice came through. "I've got eyes on you! You got them out," she exclaimed, joy evident in her tone. The distant sound of Captain Geronimo's horn filled the air in a celebratory signal.

For a split second, Tino flinched, his mind associating the sound with Lobo's vessel.

"It's all right, they're on our side," Dana assured him.

Tino cast a glance towards the boat. "Makes sense. That boat's far too nice for a scoundrel like Lobo," he remarked.

Captain Geronimo's gruff voice echoed through the radio. "The authorities won't be here for at least half an hour. That man needs urgent help. We'll get you onboard and get him to Mariposa Beach in about fifteen minutes. It's a faster way to get him aid."

Benny nodded. "Puerto Coyote, the nearest Coast Guard station, is fifty miles out. The closest police station is thirty miles out."

"At full throttle, it'd still take the Coast Guard over two hours to reach us," Ivan added.

Benny continued, "Once at Mariposa Beach, we can rush him to the Nosara clinic. They can stabilize him there and organize a transfer to the major trauma center in the city."

Consensus was swift. Dana relayed back, "We're on board with the plan, Captain."

From the boat, Courtney kept a vigilant watch for any signs of Lobo while Captain Geronimo sped towards them on his dinghy, its motor humming smoothly. It was a tiny dinghy, so given the limited space, they decided that Ina, with her Red Cross First Aid certification, should accompany Beto and monitor his condition. Dana, Benny, Ivan, and Tino remained on the sandy shore.

"I'm relieved Beto is getting help, but I can't bear the thought of leaving my birds in that cave," said Tino.

Dana stepped closer, her voice urgent. "Tino, once Lobo wraps up his deceitful paperwork to steal your land, he'll be back. We have to get out of here. The National Police and the

Coast Guard are on their way. They'll ensure the safety of your birds."

"They're right, Tino. I've spoken to the crew at the nesting area. Lobo hasn't located it yet, and it's heavily guarded for now," Ivan said.

"My truck is up at your place; it's best if we all leave until the police secure the area," Benny said.

Tino's eyes were strong, as was his resolve. "I appreciate all you've done, but I'm not leaving my home. You all go back to Mariposa Beach. I'll be fine."

Dana raised an eyebrow. "What now?"

"I've got a shotgun and a .22 rifle up at my place. This time, they won't catch me off guard. Whether they approach by water or land, I'm ready. They're in for a surprise. Think Scarface."

The gravity of the situation was palpable, but Dana couldn't stifle a smirk as she pictured Tino echoing Scarface's iconic line, "Say hello to my little friend." Yet she was acutely aware of the danger in confronting Lobo and his men. Convincing Tino to act sensibly now seemed like her most challenging task yet. His stride, steadfast and resolved, belied the harrowing ordeal he'd endured for the past three days.

Dana exchanged glances with Benny and Ivan as they all headed toward the pathway to Tino's house. Perhaps they could reason with him then to leave with them.

She watched Geronimo's boat retreat into the distance, removing their only lookout. Her radio buzzed, pulling her from her thoughts. "Dana, you're now on your own. Please, be safe and make a quick exit out of there," Courtney said.

"We're on it, Courtney," Dana responded. The breeze from the Pacific sent a chilling reminder not just of the cold, but of the looming threat that could be approaching from out there in the open water.

CHAPTER TWENTY-THREE

Navigating Tino's pathway back to the top of the cliff proved more treacherous than the way down. Dana clung to the rope for support, each movement calculated to prevent a misstep that would send her tumbling backwards. The sheer verticality of the climb was almost surreal. She wasn't exactly free-climbing El Capitan à la Alex Honnold, but she was well aware of the gravity of the situation.

The alternative to this hidden route was a thirty-minute detour around the mountain to Tino's house — a journey she shuddered to imagine during the rainy season. Thankfully, because of the pathway they reached Tino's property in a mere ten minutes.

Once at the top, Dana was relieved not to see Lobo and his henchmen there, pointing rifles at them.

Tino looked around at his place sadly. "Those no-good bums."

"We need to get moving before Lobo and his men show up," Benny said.

"I already told you. I'm not going anywhere," Tino said.

Dana's radio cracked to life. It was Courtney.

"Officer Freddy came down with a police pickup truck and he took Beto to the hospital in Nosara. He put out an urgent alert and the police are making their way down here," Courtney said.

"That's great news!" Dana replied, relieved that the police were finally taking this situation more seriously.

"Are you driving back here?"

"Not yet. We just got up here, and Tino refuses to leave."

"Well, he's a grown man, Dana. You've done all you could do. Cracked this case wide open. So if he wants to stay there and wait for Lobo, that's his prerogative. You, Benny, and Ivan should get out of there right away."

Dana mulled that over. She knew Courtney was right. So why was she still there?

"Dana!" Courtney yelped through the radio when her friend didn't reply right away.

"Sorry. You're right, let me talk to Benny."

"Okay. Get a move on, girl!"

Benny had heard the conversation. "She's right, Dana."

"I know," Dana replied.

Dana gave Tino the update on his brother. "Good. Hopefully, it's not too late for him. But I'm sure glad we ended our feud a couple of weeks ago." Tino went inside his house, inviting them all in. "I need to wash up and change out of these smelly clothes. I won't be long," he said, disappearing down a long hallway to his bedroom.

"I don't think he realizes the danger of sticking around here," Dana said.

"Well, they tied him up in a cave, they shot his brother. He knows he is just more stubborn than a mule," Benny said.

Dana, Benny, and Ivan picked up the overturned furniture that Lobo and his men had left in their wake when they attacked and kidnapped Tino.

A few minutes later, he emerged from his bedroom, freshly changed, firmly gripping a shotgun in one hand and a rifle in the other. "I intend to stand my ground. I'll defend this place until the authorities arrive. You should all head back to Mariposa Beach, where you'll be out of harm's way."

Ivan reached out and took the rifle, inspecting it. It was well-maintained. He could smell the scent of gun oil. "I served my mandatory year in the Russian army. I can manage this."

Dana peered out the window, straining to catch any signs of police lights or sirens. Life in this remote corner had always demanded self-sufficiency, but this was pushing it to the extreme. And what could she possibly contribute if Lobo returned? While Tino and Ivan were armed and adept with their weapons, she and Benny were out of their element. Urbanites thrust into a rustic showdown. She'd never even held a gun. What was she going to do, pelt them with pebbles? No, her energies would be better spent in town, pressuring the authorities to act promptly.

"All right, we're heading to Mariposa Beach. We'll do everything in our power to speed up the police's arrival. I can't fathom why they're taking their time, even considering our remote location." As Dana and Benny walked towards the SUV, a pang of guilt tugged at her heart for leaving the duo behind. "You sure you don't want to reconsider? There is plenty of space," she said with faint hope.

The determination in their eyes remained unchanged. "We're staying."

She had just swung open the SUV's door when the static from her radio interrupted her movements. Expecting Courtney, she was surprised by the unfamiliar male voice.

"You can't count on anyone coming to save you," the voice warned menacingly.

"Who are you?" Dana asked.

Before the voice could reply, Tino said grimly, "I'd know that voice anywhere. It's that fiend, Lobo."

The sinister chuckle from the radio cast a chill in the room. "Looks like someone saved you for now, old man." Lobo's tone dripped with malice. "Enjoy your last moments of freedom. I'll be seeing you shortly."

Dana tried to bluff. "The police and Coast Guard are on their way."

Lobo left the receiver open to broadcast his laughter. It sounded maniacal. Like a hyena closing in for an attack.

"Poor Dana. Captain Geronimo and his lovely companion Courtney weren't in touch with the authorities. They were speaking to me. No saviors are coming, just me and my crew."

Doubt gnawed at Dana. Could *he* be bluffing?

"And let me be clear," Lobo continued, "the only reason you're hearing this is because we're nearly there. I want you to know what awaits you for meddling in my operations and trying to rat me out. The clock's ticking."

The line went silent.

Dana looked down, her fingers gripping the radio so tightly that it shook. "Do you think he's bluffing?"

Benny hesitated. "He sounded awfully confident."

"But Courtney mentioned speaking to Officer Freddy, telling him about what happened here," Dana countered, trying to grasp any strand of hope.

"Yet Freddy assumed she also reached out to the National Police and Coast Guard. That's probably why he focused on Beto's immediate care instead of rushing here," Benny responded.

Dana's fingers flew to the radio's button, but the only response she got was relentless static. She pressed it repeatedly, her eyes widening in panic.

"Why now? Why is this malfunctioning right when we need it most?" she cried.

"It's not malfunctioning," Ivan interjected. "It's been deliberately jammed, which means they're close."

They exchanged worried glances as they rushed outside. The wild wind hit them with unbridled force, sending Dana's hair flying and whipping the loose edges of Ivan's shirt around.

Their eyes darted towards the sea, where the silhouette of a boat, dark against the horizon's waning light, bobbed gently. The vessel had an eerie aura, casting a shadow on the undulating water beneath. It was unmistakably Lobo's ship, its tall mast and rugged outline recognizable even from this distance.

They ran up to the edge of the cliff, where jagged rocks met the wrath of the sea. Below, the soft, golden sand of the beach contrasted sharply with a lone dinghy, its sides glistening from the recently completed journey.

The dinghy was empty, but a trail of footprints meandered away from it, leading ominously towards the hidden passage.

The waves crashing against the cliffs sounded almost like whispered threats, each louder and more insistent than the last. The realization, cold and stark, dawned upon them.

Dana, barely audible over the deafening roar of the ocean, captured the sentiment shared by all: "They're here!"

"Only one way they can come up here from down there, and that's through my pathway. We can ambush them!" Tino said, holding his rifle in the air like he was shaking his fist at Lobo and his men. He ran off toward the hidden hatch door.

Dana, Benny, and Ivan sprinted after Tino. As they reached the entrance, the creak of the pathway's hatch door caught their attention. Dana's heart dropped, realizing that they were too late. Their pursuers were opening the door from inside the tunnel.

Ivan and Tino aimed their weapons, but the distance made

it nearly impossible. The .22 rifle might have been good for small game, but against a group of heavily armed thugs it felt meek and inadequate — like going into battle with a BB gun. Tino racked the shotgun, but with the strong winds from the Pacific and the small pellet shotshell he had for ammunition, he couldn't do much damage to the thugs.

Before Tino or Ivan could even level their weapons, the sky became awash in a breathtaking spectrum of reds, yellows, and blues. A chorus of sharp, urgent squawks filled the air, making Dana's eardrum ache. Like the legendary Flying Tigers fighter squadron from World War II diving into battle, dozens of scarlet macaws swooped down, their vibrant plumage a blur, their intent clear and fierce.

As the hatch door was flung open, men with long guns and hard faces exited the tunnel to be met with dozens of parrots diving at them as they looked around in shock, waving their arms and protecting their heads as some of the birds used their sharp, elongated claws to strike at them.

Dana blinked, half-expecting to wake up from this bizarre turn of events, certain that she must be dreaming.

"I can't believe it," Ivan murmured, his eyes wide with astonishment as he watched the magnificent birds descend upon their foes.

Lobo's men, surprised and outmatched by the flock, flailed and screamed, trying to fend off the unexpected attackers running around as if being swarmed by bees. One henchman dropped his weapon, swatting at an aggressive macaw that had taken a liking to his long hair; it sank its claws into the man's mane and yanked as if trying to lift him into the air. Another henchman tripped over his own feet, cursing as the colorful avian defenders swarmed him. A third man fired aimlessly into the air, as yet another henchman cried in pain, "You shot me in the leg, you idiot!" The man lay on the ground holding his wound with one hand and fending off macaws with the other. It was like watching a scene from Hitchcock's, *The Birds*. And, even more amazingly, none of the parrots were attacking Dana, Benny, Ivan, and Tino. Dana couldn't believe it.

Benny couldn't suppress a laugh. "Looks like they know who the bad guys are!"

Tino's eyes gleamed with pride and admiration. "They're protecting their own. And us," he whispered, touched by the loyalty of the majestic birds.

Ivan watched with a look of utter shock. Dana imagined his scientific mind couldn't compute what he was seeing with his own eyes.

As the macaws continued their relentless assault, the group of defenders took advantage of the distraction. They approached cautiously, disarming the dazed men. The rest of the crew had had enough of the aerial assault and darted down the pathway, closing the hatch door and leaving behind the wounded man and a companion who bled from being pecked and clawed.

"No honor among thieves," Benny said.

Ivan and Benny had armed themselves with the more powerful weapons of their foes and used them to pin the men down until they could figure out their next move. Tino carefully opened the hatch door and fired a shotgun blast down just in case the men tried to come up again. That would give them second thoughts.

Dana chuckled, her nerves momentarily eased. "I think we owe these birds our lives." Her relief was palpable, as was her gratitude for the unexpected allies in their time of need.

Tino looked down at the fallen men. Neither was Lobo. "Seems your brave leader abandoned ship and left you behind," he taunted, watching the two men groan in pain, ironically over-powered and held in check by their own firearms.

As abruptly as they'd arrived, the flock disappeared, leaving an eerie stillness. The group exchanged glances, trying to process the surreal turn of events.

Ivan, still in awe, whispered to Tino, "Who needs an army when you have friends with wings?"

CHAPTER TWENTY-FOUR

Dana and Benny cautiously approached the edge of the cliff. Each step of theirs was gentle, like those of cats stalking prey, as they tried to catch a glimpse of the beach without exposing themselves to potential gunfire. The ambient noises seemed magnified — the rustling of palm leaves in rhythm with the wind and the ocean waves crashing violently against the cliff. The sounds mimicked distant gunshots.

Dana's eyes darted between the tumultuous scene below and the hatch door nearby. It felt like a grim reminder of the imminent danger they might still face from Lobo's remaining men coming back up.

Meanwhile, Ivan kept the two men left behind in check with their AR-15. And Tino, also having upgraded his weapon of choice with a machine gun he'd taken from an assailant, kept a steely grip on it, pointing it unwaveringly at the hatch. His eyes never left the door. "If it opens an inch, I'm firing away," he said nervously.

Dana watched three men tumble out of the cave below. They moved like panicked ants scrambling out of a kicked nest, darting disoriented glances around before heading toward the dinghy. They kept looking up at the cliff, probably dreading being shot with the powerful weapons they had lost. They didn't have to worry about the group above; Dana and Benny would not shoot them as long as they were running away. But Mother Nature had other plans.

And then it came, all over again, from above.

The familiar, thunderous chorus of the macaws rang out once more, the sky again assuming the glorious, brilliant colors of their feathers. The birds had found their target, this time focusing their fury on the three men below. Dive-bombing with precision, they harassed the men, their squawks mixing with the shouts and screams of their victims. Dana and Benny looked at each other in continued disbelief.

It would be comical if those three men weren't dangerous criminals — still, they were overmatched by the angry macaws.

The men desperately pushed the dinghy into the water, trying to run away from the avian assault. But the relentless macaws, sensing the men's desperation, began pecking vigorously at their heads, and then they attacked the rubber dinghy, leaving punctures in their wake.

Clumsily, the men scrambled into the deflating dinghy, paddling frantically towards the larger vessel. But as they drew further away from the shore, the dinghy lost its buoyancy thanks to the tears made into it by the parrot's claws. Dana and Benny could only watch as the deflated dinghy sank underwater.

"You're not going to believe this. The parrots attacked the men again down there. They poked holes into the dinghy, and it just sank!" Dana told Tino and Ivan.

Benny, unable to suppress a smirk at the bizarre turn of events, chimed in, "I'd wager those crooks won't be clambering up that hatch anytime soon." Encouraged by this unexpected turn of fate, Tino ventured over to join them at the cliff's edge. Together, they watched as the magnificent birds, now soaring high, converged in a vivid whirlwind of colors in celebration as the three men clung to the small part of the dinghy that wasn't underwater.

Tears shimmered in Tino's eyes, not of fear but of profound gratitude and connection with the parrots. As the flock circled above, checking on their human allies, the distinct squawks of one particular bird rang out. Dana could hear the parrot clearly shouting, *"Pillos, pillos,"* Spanish for "thieves." The two captured men, already subdued, cringed even more at the dominating presence of the birds.

"That's the talking bird from earlier, at the cave's entrance," Dana whispered in recognition.

Tino smiled widely. "Indeed. That's Baron. He was one of my very first rescues. Fifteen years ago, I came upon him. Wounded from a power line and dying. I nursed him back to health and released him to the wild," He paused, reflecting. "I named him after the Red Baron. His vivid red plumage and the way he flew, so confident and majestic, reminded me of the legendary World War I ace pilot."

A reverent hush fell upon the group as they listened, absorbing the remarkable tale. Even the two captive men seemed momentarily transported by the awe-inspiring narrative of Baron, named after the aviator considered the ace of aces in the war. And now, Baron too had proven to be a fighting bird. The ace of aces of the flock, protecting Tino and his allies.

Baron, chest puffed out in pride, gave one last sweeping glance at the motley group of humans. With an air of a job well-done, he spread his wings and took to the skies, his squadron of feathered warriors tailing him. It seemed like he was giving the signal that their mission was accomplished.

Soon after the birds took flight, the cavalry came to the rescue. Although Lobo might have tricked Courtney and Captain Geronimo into not calling the police, he didn't stop Officer Freddy from calling for backup. And Freddy had delivered! From the Pacific Ocean, two Coast Guard cutters arrived with guardsmen manning the big turret guns of the ship. And from the main road, a convoy of National Police trucks and an OIJ swat team sprang into the action.

They placed the two wounded men under arrest. Ivan, finally able to relax, joined Dana, Benny, and Tino at the cliff's edge. They could hear the coast guardsman shouting instructions through a bullhorn to the three men who floundered in the water, holding to what was left of the dinghy.

She watched as the guardsmen carefully brought the men aboard under cover of several other guardsmen, their assault rifles trained on the smugglers. The other Coast Guard ship took control of Lobo's boat.

Dana gave a sigh of relief, and Benny put his arms around her. She melted into his chest. "We're finally safe," she said once all the bad guys were under arrest.

Something out on the water caught Benny's attention. Then he laughed.

"What is it?" Dana asked.

"Take a look," he said, pointing out to sea.

Behind the two large Coast Guard ships was Captain Geronimo's boat. She could see a tiny Courtney on the deck, jumping up and down and waving at her. Dana smiled and waved back. There were other people on board, so she borrowed Ivan's binoculars to get a better look.

"Oh, my, that's some reception," Dana said.

Standing next to Courtney were Mindy, Leo, and Big Mike. The protective Ark Row merchant posse. She laughed at that, then felt a tear trickling down her cheek. It was a happy tear for the friends she had, new and old.

CHAPTER TWENTY-FIVE

IVAN REJOINED HIS TEAM OF ORNITHOLOGISTS SO THEY could figure out how to recover Tino's stolen parrots after all the adventurers made plans to meet the next evening for a celebratory dinner.

As soon as Dana and Benny drove down Main Street, the atmosphere was electric, almost like the aftermath of a victorious championship game. Word of their escapade at Tino's cove had traveled fast, spreading like wildfire through the grapevine of the small community.

Approaching Ark Row, they were met with an impromptu welcome-back brigade. Benny's truck had barely come to a halt before a sea of familiar faces surrounded them to deliver a tidal wave of warmth and concern.

In the bustling heart of the town square, Mayor Plaza was a beacon of joviality, his wide grin almost outshining the afternoon sun. Even Doña Amada, notorious for her perpetual scowl, seemed to soften a shade, her features relaxing into what could pass for a contented expression in her world. But amid the hum of the gathering, it was Courtney's warm embrace that enveloped Dana first. With a heartfelt squeeze mirroring Courtney's own, Dana found an unspoken understanding in their tight embrace, a bond between best friends that elevated to sisterhood.

"Promise me you won't give me another scare like that," Courtney whispered, pulling back to flash a relieved grin.

"I'm so sorry, Court," Dana replied, her voice catching with emotion. "Their interference with the radio made communication impossible. I tried, I swear."

Courtney nodded, her eyes misty. "Captain Geronimo suspected as much. Then he figured out that Lobo had tricked us into thinking we were talking with the police when it was him. That's when we realized the gravity of the situation and prompted the authorities into high alert."

"I can't thank you enough for rallying everyone."

"From what I've heard, you all seemed to have everything in hand. A sinking dinghy, two injured thugs at Tino's? When did you turn into an action hero?" Courtney asked playfully.

Dana chuckled. "Trust me, that wasn't us. We had some... aerial support."

"You mean like backup from the sky?"

"You could say that. I'll fill you in when we're back home. I hardly believe what happened out there, and I saw it with my own eyes."

ON THEIR DRIVE BACK, Benny voiced his concerns. "If we tell them about the scarlet macaws swooping in to save the day, they'll think we're making it up."

Dana nodded in agreement. "It sounds unbelievable, even though it's true."

"Next thing we know, they'll be checking us into Chapuí."

Benny was referring to the notorious psychiatric hospital in San José.

As the SUV traveled the long driveway to Casa Verde, Dana saw Ramon and Carmen Villalobos standing outside, clearly awaiting their arrival. Their faces were lined with worry, reflecting the unease they must have felt when they found out about Dana's ordeal. "Looks like the word spread all the way here, too," Benny remarked with a wry smile.

Dana had grown exceptionally close to Ramon and Carmen over the past seven months. When she first inherited the property from her uncle, the stipulation that it came with live-in caretakers had seemed unusual. Her uncle's will was explicit: If she accepted the property, she would also have to let Ramon and Carmen live in their modest home about half a mile from the main house.

Initially, Dana had been unsure about this arrangement. She had had a housecleaning service back in San Francisco, but they came once a month for a couple of hours. This seemed a bit much to her, but she respected her uncle's wishes. But now, after getting to know the couple and experiencing their kindness, she couldn't fathom her life at Mariposa Beach without them. They had seamlessly weaved into the fabric of her daily life, evolving from mere caretakers to treasured family members.

They were also skilled landscapers, maintaining the property with meticulous care, ensuring the vegetable garden thrived, and tending to the mango, cas, and banana trees that always bore abundant fruit. With her culinary prowess, Carmen frequently cooked traditional Costa Rican dishes that tantalized Dana's taste buds.

As the SUV pulled to a stop, Dana stepped out, her shoes crunching on the gravel pathway. She was immediately enveloped in a warm embrace by Carmen. Ramon, in his usual stoic manner, looked her up and down, ensuring she was in one piece.

"We heard about everything in town," Carmen said, her voice shaking slightly. "I was shopping for ingredients when word got around. My heart nearly stopped. Lobo is *muy malo* — a wicked man."

Dana gently pulled back, offering a reassuring smile. "I'm okay, Carmen. Really, it was intense, but I'm fine. Thanks to some unexpected help," Dana glanced over at Benny and smiled.

"I guess I'm just chopped liver, then?" Courtney said with a smirk, ever the joker.

Carmen chuckled lightly, shaking her head. "We're relieved you're all safe."

Ramon finally spoke, his voice low and humble as usual but filled with concern, "We were worried sick. This place wouldn't be the same without you."

She nodded, touched by his rare show of emotion. "Thank you, Ramon. I'm just glad to be back home."

"Your bird scientist friends came by and picked up Tino's dog, just as you asked." Ramon informed her.

"Great news. Tino will want to be reunited with his beloved Ringo." Dana smiled as she imagined the heartwarming reunion between Tino and Ringo after their three-day separation.

Carmen interjected, "You must be hungry after such a day. I've made you some black bean soup. It's on the stove, kept warm. It's just what you need to rebuild your strength."

Dana's stomach growled in agreement, making them all chuckle. "I can't argue with my stomach," she said, a little embarrassed.

THE TRIO WENT INSIDE, and the inviting aroma of homemade black bean soup enveloped them. The scent was both comforting and tantalizing, and Dana felt a warmth spread through her that had nothing to do with the tropical climate.

"Wow, Carmen really outdid herself," Courtney remarked as she breathed in the aroma.

Wally appeared out of thin air, meowing as he nuzzled Dana's legs. She crouched to greet her feline friend, who paid no mind to Benny or Courtney. "Sorry for ignoring you these past few days," Dana said. The loud purring suggested that Dana was forgiven.

She moved to the kitchen counter and lifted a cloth, revealing a thick stack of handmade corn tortillas. The tortillas were still warm to the touch, their edges slightly crisp. Carmen never bought tortillas, always insisting on making them from scratch. Dana didn't argue. Everything made at home from scratch tasted better.

Beside the tortillas, there was a big bag of crispy tostada chips. Dana could already imagine crumbling them over the soup for the perfect crunchy contrast to its rich and creamy texture. A small bowl of white rice and a bowl of *natilla* — Costa Rica's tangy, creamy answer to sour cream — completed the meal.

Benny, unable to resist any longer, reached for the lid of the soup pot and slowly lifted it. It filled the room with a rich aroma, and the sight inside the pot was truly mouthwatering. Three perfectly poached eggs, their yolks a shimmering orange, floated atop the deep black of the soup.

After indulging in their meal and savoring the cold refreshment of Imperial beer, the three of them made their way to the veranda to relax.

The darkness had completely settled though it was only six p.m., as it does every day in Costa Rica. In such tranquility, it was difficult for Dana to reconcile the idea that individuals like Lobo existed.

Dana wondered how Tino and Beto were holding up. She hadn't been able to get an update on Beto's condition. She hoped he was recovering now that he had proper medical care.

"What happens now?" Courtney asked.

Almost on cue, Dana's phone buzzed. The text message was from Detective Rojas. "Well, to begin with, the police need our statements. Detective Picado and Rojas will meet us at the bookstore at nine tomorrow morning."

CHAPTER TWENTY-SIX

DANA'S STRESSFUL DAY, COMBINED WITH THE ANTICIPATION of being interrogated by Detective Picado the following morning, resulted in a restless night. Every time she tried to find a comfortable position, Wally would shift with a low grunt. And if that wasn't enough, Elvis, the nocturnal howler monkey, did justice to his species by belting out an all-night performance.

Despite the ruckus, Dana eventually found sleep, but it was short-lived. The jarring ring of her phone jerked her awake, making her feel as if a sledgehammer was going off in the middle of the room. Squinting against the early morning light, she saw it was just past six. Who could be calling at this hour? As she picked up the phone, she didn't recognize the number.

"Hello?" Dana mumbled, rubbing her eyes.

"Dana, it's Kathy Hixson. We met a few days ago," came the reply.

Dana remembered meeting Kathy with Ina at the Airbnb rental before finding out they were ornithologists. She was the redhead.

"Yes, Kathy, I remember. Everything okay?"

Kathy hesitated for a moment. "Sorry for calling so early, but..."

"No worries. What's going on?" Dana asked, worried.

"It's about Ivan. He went over to the cove with doctors Tony Smith, Wilmer Rincon, and Ina Esser. They were helping Tino with moving the birds back to the aviary. But when they arrived, every single bird was missing. We're worried. Do you think Lobo might have gotten out on bail?"

"I'll get in touch with a detective I know and see what I can find out," Dana replied.

She quickly sent a text to Rojas, inquiring about the missing birds and if there was a possibility of Lobo being out on bail. After a brief wait, her phone buzzed with Rojas's response.

The birds? I wasn't aware. As for Lobo, he and his gang are locked up tight. Even the one who took a bullet to the leg. They're not getting a taste of freedom anytime soon.

Confused, Dana typed back.

Did the OIJ possibly move the birds?

Rojas's reply came swiftly.

No. Tino was authorized to move the birds back to his aviary to be under his care.

Dana promptly dialed Kathy Hixson to relay the news. "The birds were not taken by the OIJ and Lobo's gang is still incarcerated."

Kathy sighed heavily on the other end. "Thanks for the update. I'll get in touch with Ivan at Tino's place," she said before quickly ending the call.

Courtney, bleary-eyed from her own restless night, walked into Dana's room. "Is everything all right?"

Now fully upright in her bed, Dana frowned. "Something's not adding up."

"What's happened?" Courtney sat at the foot of Dana's bed.

"Dr. Kathy Hixson called to say that Ivan called her from

Tino's place. That the birds are still missing. She wanted to know if the police were involved and if Lobo was still in jail. So I checked with Detective Rojas and they didn't take the birds, nor did they release Lobo or his men from jail."

"That's good, isn't it?"

"That's what's puzzling. Tino's place is off the grid. No landline, no cell reception. So how could Ivan call her from there?"

"Maybe she meant to say over one of those two-way radios like were using."

Dana looked at her caller ID. The call from Kathy Hixson came from an unknown number. She called the landline of their Airbnb. It rang several times before a groggy, thick-accented voice answered, "Hello? Who is it?"

She recognized Ivan's Russian accent immediately. He sounded like he had been deep in sleep, not actively working at Tino's property as Kathy had claimed.

She relayed Kathy's message to him.

"What? That's news to me," Ivan exclaimed in surprise. "We safely transferred the birds from the cave to Tino's aviary this afternoon. Everyone's been resting here since then. None of us are up at Tino's place."

"Why would Kathy tell me all these lies?" Dana asked.

A sigh came from the other end. "Let me ask her what the heck is going on. Hold on." Dana could hear the phone rustling, then footsteps, followed by the sound of soft knocks on a door. "Kathy? It's Ivan. Can you open up?" Silence greeted him. His knocks became more insistent, but to no avail. Dana then heard a door creaking open, and a concerned Ivan said, "Kathy?"

Ivan returned to talk to Dana, more anxious than before.

"She isn't in her room. And it doesn't look like she slept here." On the other side there was the murmur of voices and footsteps. "Herman Erbel isn't here either. His bed's untouched."

"What are they up to?"

"I'm not entirely sure. But, to be honest, Kathy's been problematic throughout our stay. She's always avoiding work, grumbling about everything, and often bringing up her overwhelming college debt."

Dana's mind raced. "Could they have planned to nab the birds on their own to sell them to the black market, especially after learning about Lobo's imprisonment?"

Ivan hesitated. "Earlier, I'd have said it was impossible. But now... Still, those birds are safe at Tino's. There is no way they could sneak in and take them under his nose, and I can't fathom them using Lobo's rough-handed tactics. They're bird scientists, after all."

A thought struck Dana. "What about the nesting area? That's miles from Tino's house."

"They wouldn't dare..." Ivan said after gasping.

"What wouldn't they dare, Ivan?"

His voice, filled with urgency, replied, "Meet us at Tino's *pronto*. We need to see for ourselves."

BENNY PULLED up just a few minutes after Dana and Courtney finished getting ready. Dana passed a warm coffee tumbler to Courtney and another to Benny. He yawned, gratefully accepting the java.

"Oh, perfect timing," he mumbled, rubbing the sleep from his eyes. "I had every intention of heading back to the city after our police meeting later. Was banking on a few more hours of sleep. This should help." He took a long sip and smiled. "Just like I like it, thanks."

"I know just how much half-and-half you take with your coffee. Sorry for dragging you to Tino's place yet again."

"Funny how life works, huh? Haven't been to that area in ages, and now it's become an almost daily trip."

Courtney shook her head, her brow furrowed in confusion. "Wait, so let me get this straight. These ornithologists — they went rogue and stole the very birds they were supposed to rescue?"

Dana shrugged, her expression troubled. "That's what it's looking like. Kathy Hixson wasn't there for the actual rescue. She claimed to be ill. Food poisoning from bad ceviche."

"If she's planning on selling the birds in the black market, how would she even have the connections?" Benny asked.

"Ivan mentioned that was her area of expertise. She did her PhD research on the effects of the black market on bird populations. She'd have insider knowledge and understand the intricacies of it all. Without Lobo in the picture, she can operate with no middleman to cut into her profits, and she won't risk crossing him on his turf since he's behind bars."

"I never knew the study and preservation of birds could be this dangerous, with smugglers and rogue scientists running amok," Courtney said.

Dana just hoped they could figure out what Kathy was up to with enough time to stop it.

CHAPTER TWENTY-SEVEN

THE MORNING SUN WAS JUST BEGINNING TO FILTER through the dense foliage when Dana, Benny, and Courtney arrived at Tino's. The homestead, usually full of birdcalls, felt eerily quiet, as if the animals could sense the tension among the humans.

Ivan and the rest of his team were gathered outside Tino's place. As Dana approached, Ina broke away from the group and met her halfway.

"All the birds from Tino's aviary are safe," she said, sounding relieved.

"Good," Dana replied. "What about the nesting spot?"

"That's where we're headed next," Ivan said, joining them.

Tino, overhearing the conversation, waved them over. "The spot is deep within the woods, a small clearing that the birds favor. I'll stay here just in case they try to make another move against my friends in the aviary," Tino said, holding his trusty shotgun. Tony Smith, the ornithologist from Cornell, stayed with Tino to help him if needed.

The rest of the group, led by Ivan, set off. The path was narrow, winding its way through dense vegetation and overgrown roots. Now and then, a bird would fly overhead as if they were checking up on the humans.

The humid air was thickening with the earthy aroma of damp soil and the sweet smell of blossoming trees.

As they trudged on, their sense of unease grew. The reality of what Kathy and Herman might have done weighed heavily on everyone's mind. "If they've disturbed the nesting site, the consequences could be dire," Ina told Dana with concern. "Long-lasting damage could be done once people get their grubby hands into a nest."

About twenty minutes into their hike, the trees thinned out, revealing a serene clearing. The first thing that caught Dana's eye was the grandeur of the nesting site. It was nature's spectacle: a myriad bird species nested here, their vibrant colors creating a mosaic against the backdrop of the lush rainforest.

But something was amiss.

The ground was scattered with remnants of broken twigs and footprints that hadn't been there the last time Ivan visited. The nests seemed undisturbed at first glance, but a closer look revealed empty spaces where eggs once lay.

Ivan kneeled, examining the footprints. "There were definitely two people here. These prints... they match the type of boots we wear out here."

"So they did come," Dana said.

Visibly distressed, Ivan said, "I never thought bird scientists would stoop this low."

Benny added, "Desperation makes people do unthinkable things."

They stood in silence, processing the implications of the theft. It was clear now that Kathy and Herman had targeted something far more precious than the group had initially thought: the actual eggs.

THE GROUP SPED through the dense undergrowth towards the main road.

"They've got to have a vehicle," Ivan gasped as he ran. "They planned this. There's no way they're going to flee on foot."

As they approached the road's edge, a cacophony of sounds assaulted their ears — tires screeching, the roar of an engine, and a man's voice echoing through the trees and shouting, "Kathy, wait up!"

"That's Herman's voice!" Ivan exclaimed, running faster.

They burst onto the road just in time to see the tail end of a car disappearing around a bend. Dust and loose gravel flew in its wake. Once the air cleared, they noticed Dr. Herman Erbel standing on the road alone, looking dazed and lost as the car sped away without him.

Dana recognized Herman. He was the one with the hipster beard standing next to Kathy on her security video. The one who kept checking his watch. These two had been planning this heist for a while.

"What's going on, Herman?" Ivan demanded.

Herman slowly turned, surprise registering on his face when he saw all of them standing there, looking at him with disappointment and anger. His eyes welled up and tears streamed down his face.

"You're one of us, Herman. How could you betray everything we stand for?" Ina exclaimed.

"And rob our forests of its precious treasure," added Wilmer Rincon.

"All for a little money," Ivan said.

Herman gulped back his tears, his voice shaking. "It's not what you think."

Ivan stepped closer. "Then enlighten us. Did you decide those eggs were your golden ticket?"

Herman's gaze dropped to the ground, and he whispered, "It wasn't for me. It was for her."

Dana and Ivan exchanged puzzled glances.

"You're in love with her, aren't you?" Dana said. It seemed that Kathy had played Herman like a sad fiddle.

He nodded, tears streaming afresh. "Yes. I love Kathy. She was drowning in debt. I thought... I thought if I helped her, she'd—"

"She'd love you back?" Benny interjected, looking both sympathetic and disgusted. "And instead, she left you here."

"Abandoned on the side of the road after using you," Courtney added. "That's one cold chick."

The weight of his choices crashed down on Herman. "She promised. She said she loved me. But I was just a tool to her. What have I done? I've ruined my career and pushed that endangered species further into extinction."

Ivan told Herman it was best if he stayed clear of Tino and his shotgun after what he had done.

"So where is she headed to?" Dana asked Herman.

"She didn't tell me that. Just that we were going to meet with a broker in a couple hours to sell the eggs."

"She needs to smuggle those eggs out of the country. That's not a simple task. But she must have planned to meet the buyer somewhere around here," Ivan said.

"Costa Rica has strict laws on smuggling protected wildlife like those macaws. There is no way she's going on an airplane," Benny said.

"She's probably headed to the Panama border. Huge black market over there. It's a busy hub for many illicit goods," Benny said. "Paso Canoas is the main border crossing between Costa

Rica and Panama. It's pretty rustic, but it's the best way to cross by land, and it's only a ninety-minute drive from here."

Wilmer Rincon stayed with Herman on the side of the road while the rest of the group hiked back to Tino's to get Benny's truck. Dana made them pick up their pace, desperate to get into cellphone range so she could call Detective Rojas. The police might be able to stop Kathy before she crossed the border into Panama.

BACK AT TINO'S, Ivan briefly explained what was going on as Ivan and Ina joined Dana and Courtney in Benny's SUV.

Tony agreed to pick up Wilmer and Herman in his rental and take them to Mariposa Beach. Benny took off down the road, driving fast after Kathy Hixson. Dana was resolved to not let her get away with this crime.

CHAPTER TWENTY-EIGHT

The narrow road winded through the forest. The dense foliage on both sides created the illusion of traveling through a green tunnel.

As Benny drove down the twisty road, they were met with a brilliant flash of red-feathered birds flying over them. Another flock of parrots.

They watched, stunned, as the flock of scarlet macaws soared overhead. Among the loud squawks they heard the distinct sound of the talking parrot echoing, *"Pillo, pillo...* thief, thief."

Benny slowed the car, and their eyes tracked the parrots as they flew away. He continued driving slowly until coming upon a crumbled car in the ditch just ahead. Smoke rose from the engine.

He parked swiftly, and the group rushed towards the wreckage. They found Kathy Hixson inside the vehicle, her head leaning against the deflated airbag, a trail of blood oozing down her forehead.

Ivan, bending into the car's shattered window, called out, "Kathy! Kathy, are you okay?"

Kathy's eyelids fluttered open, and her gaze was unfocused. She winced as she touched her bloodied forehead. "The parrots... they... they came from nowhere. I couldn't see..." she whispered, trying to recall. "I swerved... and they... they ran me off the road."

Dana bent down beside Ivan, looking into the wreckage. "They did it again. How is this possible?" she asked.

Still processing the scene, Ivan shook his head. "I can't even begin to understand what's happening here with these parrots."

As they worked to get Kathy out of the wrecked vehicle, the distant caw of the parrots resonated in the background, a reminder of nature's unpredictable power.

Ina checked on Kathy. "She's concussed. One or two broken ribs. But not bad, considering."

Ivan looked inside the mangled car for the eggs but couldn't find them. He popped the trunk. Kathy's suitcase was there. He opened it and rifled through it, but no eggs.

"Where are they, Kathy?" Ivan asked; he couldn't hide his anger over what she had done.

But she didn't reply. After studying the trunk, Dana pulled back the lining and removed the cardboard cutout to access the spot where one would find the spare tire and jack. Near the side by the back, there was a box.

"That's it," Ivan said, looking over her shoulder. He carefully removed it. "This is a specialized cooler for transporting eggs for incubation. This wasn't a spur-of-the-moment thing for her. She planned this well."

Ivan inspected the box with Ina.

"Oh, thank goodness, none of the eggs were damaged," Ina said, relieved.

The ornithologists gave high-fives to Dana, Benny, and Courtney, as well as each other.

"I'm not sure what's going on, but it looks like good news," a confused Courtney said as everyone laughed.

"It's wonderful news. We can return these eggs back to where they belong, safely," Ivan said.

A FEW MINUTES LATER, Tony and Wilmer drove up with Herman in the backseat. He looked out, wide-eyed, and became distraught when he saw the injured Kathy sitting on the side of the road next to the damaged vehicle.

Though she had ditched him and his feelings for Kathy were obviously much stronger than anything she felt for him — and he must have realized all this — he was still worried about her.

Love is strange, Dana thought, witnessing the sad reunion between Herman and Kathy.

THEY WAITED for about twenty more minutes, until they heard the unmistakable wail of sirens piercing the quiet air. The sirens were distant at first, but grew steadily louder, signaling the approach of the authorities. The dense canopy of the forest was intermittently lit by the blue and red flashes from the police vehicles. Detective Rojas and Picado had already arrived in Mariposa Beach to interview Dana and the others about the Lobo case, so they were able to get there much faster than if they were coming from their regular posting at the OIJ station in Nicoya.

Detective Picado and Rojas stepped out of the lead car, their demeanor stern and assertive. A duo of uniformed officers followed them. Rojas quickly assessed the situation, her eyes flitting between the damaged car, Kathy's dazed form, and the group standing a short distance away. Picado walked up to the group.

"What happened here?" he demanded, looking at Dana.

Why me? she wondered. Well, she knew the answer since whenever trouble arose around Mariposa Beach, she seemed to be in the thick of it — much to Picado's chagrin.

Dana recounted the events, emphasizing Kathy's and Herman's role in the theft of the parrot eggs and explaining the unexpected interference from the parrots that caused Kathy to wreck the car. Picado and Rojas listened intently, occasionally glancing at each other and at the wreckage.

"The parrots did what?" an incredulous Picado asked.

Ivan, Benny, and even the injured Kathy confirmed how the birds had swarmed Kathy as she drove, causing her to swerve and crash.

Picado and Rojas glanced at each other like Joe Friday and Bill Gannon on *Dragnet*. They must think we're all nuts, Dana thought, but that's what happened.

Picado placed Kathy and Herman under arrest for violating the endangered species act, theft, endangerment — and probably even more charges later, he warned.

Herman went straight to jail. Kathy would make a pit stop at the hospital for her concussion and broken ribs before heading to jail as well.

Dana watched the police take the two ornithologists away. There was more sadness than happiness this time; Lobo and his men were long-time career criminals doing what was expected of them. But Kathy Hixson and Herman Ebell were ornithologists supposed to care for and protect the parrots, not break wildlife protection laws to smuggle and profit from them. Their actions hurt more than Lobo's.

And Dana could see from the grave expression on the other ornithologists' faces that they took the betrayal personally. As if the dastardly deeds of Kathy and Herman would attach themselves to them within their community.

CHAPTER TWENTY-NINE

As the sun dipped below the horizon, the Que Vista restaurant came alive, bathed in the soft glow of lights woven around the thatched roof of the palapa. Tiki torches mounted on bamboo sticks dotted the sands, casting a warm, flickering light and adding to the enchantment. A cherished spot for both locals and visitors where the gentle lull of waves met the shore, accompanied by the mellow tunes playing in the background and crafting a serene ambiance for the evening.

Maria Rivera had reserved the best table for a special gathering. This table was right on the beach under an elegant thatch-roof palapa offering a panoramic view of the expansive ocean and allowing the gentle sea breeze to refresh its occupants.

It was the celebratory dinner with the ornithologists. They were all supposed to get together the night before, but Kathy Hixson and Herman Erbil had put the kibosh on those plans. But now they were trying again.

Dana, Benny, and Courtney had arrived first. They chatted and laughed, reminiscing about their recent adventures. Soon enough, Ina Esser, Wilmer Rincon, and Tony

Smith joined, their arrival amplifying the joy and camaraderie of the group.

As conversations flowed and they poured drinks, all heads turned to the entrance when Ivan showed up with a surprise guest: Tino. For those who knew Tino's reclusive nature, seeing him here was nothing short of astonishing. Even the staff, familiar with the stories of the enigmatic and eccentric bird lover, exchanged surprised and excited glances at seeing him at the restaurant.

Dana's face lit up the brightest. "Tino! I can't believe you're here," she exclaimed, rising from her seat to greet him with a hug.

Tino, a man of few words, just smiled and nodded, clearly overwhelmed but happy. "It's the least I could do. To show my appreciation," he said simply.

Tino looked good, all things considered, but the physical signs of his harrowing ordeal were still evident. Dark bruises, varying from purples to yellows, marred his face and arms, and there was a slight hesitation in his steps, each one deliberate and cautious. His eyes, though, held a resilience that was unmistakable.

He took a seat, wincing slightly as he adjusted his position. Everyone at the table could sense his discomfort, but Tino, ever the stoic, tried to downplay his injuries with a small smile.

"I'm doing much better, really," Tino assured them, seeing their concerned glances. "A few more days, and I'll be back to my old self."

A familiar bark suddenly interrupted the soft chatter of the restaurant as Ringo ran out on the beach, his tail wagging so fast it was almost a blur. Without hesitation, he made a beeline for Dana, barking joyfully and nuzzling her legs, showering her with doggy affection.

"Ringo!" Dana exclaimed with delight, bending down to

scratch the exuberant dog behind his ears. "You sure missed me, didn't you?"

Tino laughed. "Looks like Ringo wanted to thank you for all the treats and attention you gave him while I was away. Thank you for taking care of my boy."

"It was my pleasure," Dana said.

Ringo, feeling the energy of the beach calling him again, darted around the tables. His four paws kicked up small flurries of sand as he sped up and down the shoreline. While the sea beckoned, Ringo was content to race along the edge, playfully darting in and out of breaking waves as they chased him away.

As the evening wore on and plates of delicious Costa Rican fare appeared on the table, Ringo's energy waned. His runs became trots, and his trots became slow walks. By the time the main course was being served, an exhausted Ringo had meandered back to Tino's side, giving a long, satisfied stretch before curling up at his feet and crashing.

Dana chuckled. "Looks like someone's had a full day."

Tino smiled fondly at his loyal companion. "He sure has. But what better place to relax after a run than here?"

And with that, under the starlit sky and the gentle serenade of waves, Ringo's soft snores became a soothing backdrop to the night's conversation.

Maria Rivera and her staff had delivered quite the feast. The aroma of fried whole fish mingled with the salty scent of the sea. Bowls of seafood rice, plates of fried garlic yucca, heart of palm salad, and the essential sides of rice, beans, and tortillas filled the table, embodying the rich culinary heritage of Costa Rica.

Two pitchers of ice-cold mango daiquiri sat in the middle of the table.

Lifting his glass, Ivan said, "To new beginnings, to the birds we saved, and to justice!"

They met the toast with a chorus of cheers, the group's laughter blending seamlessly with the music and the murmur of the waves. The evening, filled with joy and camaraderie, was a testament to their collective journey, one that had brought them closer together.

Dana watched the waves rhythmically crash onto the shoreline, their repetitive motion having a strangely calming effect on her. The beachfront dinner was turning out to be a night of celebration and reflection. Yet, amidst all the jubilation, she couldn't help but think about the person missing from the gathering.

She turned to Tino, who sat contemplatively sipping his drink. "Tino," she began, choosing her words carefully, "How is your brother doing? I've been thinking about him since the day of the rescue."

Tino looked up, clearly touched by her concern. "Thank you for asking, Dana. He's in San José, at the hospital. The latest update I got was quite positive. He's awake, alert, and seems to be in good spirits. They say he's recovering faster than they had expected. In fact, they plan on discharging him in a couple of days. His daughter and her family are taking good care of him."

Dana smiled, genuinely relieved. "That's wonderful news, Tino. He's clearly a fighter, just like you."

His lips curled into a slight smile. "He's always been the resilient one. I'm just glad he's on the mend. It's been a trying time for his family. And I'm looking forward to continuing our reconciliation after years of estrangement."

"I can only imagine," Dana said. "But now, with all the culprits behind bars and the birds safe, I hope both of you can find some peace."

"One step at a time, Dana. One step at a time."

Dana could feel the weight of Tino's unspoken guilt. His brother had been injured, racing against time and danger to save

Tino from Lobo's clutches. The lines on Tino's face, deepened by worry, told a story of responsibility and regret.

Her eyes shifted to Courtney. The thought of the perils she had exposed her friend to gnawed at Dana. And Benny... he had been right beside them, facing the same risks. The burden of leading her friends into danger was something she felt deeply.

Though worlds apart, Tino's reclusive life in the woods and her own relentless pursuit of truth seemed to converge on one thing: a stubborn determination that often came at a personal cost. The understanding of their shared nature hung between them, unspoken but palpable.

"Did you manage to safely return the eggs?" Courtney asked.

Ivan nodded with a hint of pride. "Yes, they're right back in their rightful place. Tino has painstakingly built a haven for these rare parrots. It's heartbreaking to think that their numbers are dwindling so rapidly in the wild. But thanks to Tino's work, this area of Morpho Bay is one of the preeminent spots to view these beautiful creatures in their natural habitat."

Dana hesitated, glancing around at the group. They were all engrossed in their conversations, but she sensed everyone was avoiding a particular topic. Taking a deep breath, she seized the opportunity, knowing this might be her only chance to discuss it with such a distinguished group of ornithologists. "About the Baron's aerial assaults on the bad guys... How did that even happen? Three times?"

Ivan paused to consider Dana's question. He rubbed his shaved head as he looked out at the horizon, deep in thought.

"Truthfully, Dana, there's no scientific evidence to suggest that macaws possess that level of strategic intelligence," Ivan began. "Sure, they're clever birds. They can mimic sounds, solve problems, and even use tools. But planning and executing aerial attacks in the way we witnessed ... well, that's something we've never observed or documented."

Dana frowned. "So, you're saying it's just a coincidence?"

"Many in the scientific community would be quick to dismiss it as such. The narrative would be that we're just reading too much into random bird behavior, anthropomorphizing them."

"But you were there, Ivan. You saw it happen. Do you believe it was just mere coincidence?"

Ivan took another moment before answering. "Coincidence or not, I cannot deny what I witnessed. It was something extraordinary and entirely unexpected. I've dedicated my life to studying these magnificent creatures, and just when I thought I had a good grasp on their behaviors and capabilities, they surprised me."

He looked around at the table, his gaze settling on Tino, who was silently listening.

"I've decided that my new life's work will be understanding this phenomenon. There's so much we don't know about the macaws' cognitive abilities, and if there's even a slight chance that they acted in the way we saw deliberately, then it's worth exploring."

Dana smiled, admiration in her eyes. "That's commendable, Ivan. You might just rewrite the books on avian intelligence."

"Or become the laughingstock of the ornithological community. But I've always believed that genuine discovery lies in chasing the mysteries, not in sticking to what's already known."

CHAPTER THIRTY

EPILOGUE

AFTER EVERYTHING THAT HAD HAPPENED, DANA AND Benny were determined to ensure that Courtney's last days in Mariposa Beach were full of fun and relaxation under the tropical sun, without the lingering tension and dangers from their recent escapades.

Dana was more than happy to put her days of battling smugglers and rescuing stolen exotic birds behind her. Time to just be a beach bum. And more importantly, she wanted to show Courtney the good time she had promised before her friend flew down from San Francisco, only to get her mixed up in the whole Lobo mess.

Dana and Courtney did yoga at Jai Das's Transformation Institute, a holistic retreat perched above the rugged oceanside bluffs of Mariposa Beach a few miles from Casa Verde. Afterwards, they ambled on the sandy shores, letting the waves kiss their feet. They drove up to Arenal, where the trio then reveled in the soothing balmy waters of the Tabacón hot springs, basking in the natural warmth provided by the Arenal volcano's underground thermal activity where they could smell the sulfur in the air.

On Courtney's last day in town, Dana was sad driving her to the Daniel Oduber Quirós International Airport in Liberia for her flight back to the US. She would miss her friend. But she also felt content because she had made new friends at Mariposa Beach.

As the days blended into weeks, more intricate details about the entire bird debacle emerged. Dana, settled back into her regular routine was privy to what had gone down in that sordid underbelly of the smuggling operation they had disrupted.

Kathy Hixson, driven not by remorse but by the allure of a lighter sentence became the prosecution's star witness, providing invaluable information that helped to shut down an even larger smuggling ring than Lobo's in David, Panama. The collaborative sting operation, set up by Interpol with Costa Rican and Panamanian agents, had Kathy in the role of an informant, wired and ready to expose the illicit network.

Detective Rojas filled Dana in on the aftermath. "Considering Kathy's cooperation and her being a first-time offender, she's looking at a hefty fine followed by deportation and a lifetime ban from entering Costa Rica. But no prison time."

Dana mused on the irony of Kathy's actions. *Stealing those eggs to clear debts, only to accumulate more in the end.*

Ivan had told Dana that although Kathy would pay for her crimes in Costa Rica with the fine and deportation but no serious jail time, in the ornithological community her punishment would be much stiffer for a scientist like Kathy. The American Ornithological Society voted to permanently expel her from amongst their ranks and word was that Cornell University had fired her. Her life as a respected ornithologist was over.

Costa Rican officials also fined, then deported Herman back

to his home country of Germany, where he would face the same fate as Kathy from the local ornithological community and academia. He too was banned from coming back to Costa Rica.

The fate of Lobo and his gang was a different story when it came to prison time. While the wheels of Costa Rican justice turned slowly, they were grinding inexorably towards a guilty verdict. Lobo's underlings, like rats fleeing a sinking ship, were ready to testify against their boss. Considering Lobo's rap sheet, he was on a one-way trip to a lengthy prison stay.

Dana remarked to Tino, "Lobo's caged, much like those birds he locked up. We won't be hearing from him anytime soon."

Tino's sanctuary was the silver lining of this ordeal. Ivan helped him establish the Baron Aviary Foundation to make his contribution to helping his beloved birds official. The Costa Rican government and the American and German ornithological societies had provided hefty grants so he could continue his work. That financial windfall meant Tino could continue saving and helping parrots even more.

BACK IN CASA VERDE, the sun was setting, casting its orange glow over Mariposa Beach as the last rays danced on the water. The sea seemed to glisten in the twilight. The ambiance was perfect for a peaceful evening at home, and after the last hectic couple of weeks, Dana and Benny were ready to enjoy every bit of it.

Carmen's culinary prowess was unparalleled, and this evening's meal was yet another testament to that. A simmering pot of *chifrijo* waited for them. The inviting aroma of steaming beans perfectly complemented the rich scent of the *chicharrón* (pork belly), instantly igniting one's appetite. The chimichurri sauce looked vibrant and fresh. It added a zest to the food, while the chili peppers promised some heat. To balance it all out, the tortilla chips provided a delightful crunch against the soft, fluffy white rice that would serve as accompaniment.

Dana and Benny, unable to resist any longer, ladled generous servings of the *chifrijo* into their bowls, ready to be washed down with an ice-cold bottle of Imperial beer.

They went up to Dana's sanctuary, the wrap-around veranda with breathtaking views of Mariposa Beach. They enjoyed spending time together as Wally eyed them, hoping for some of that *chicharrón*. He meowed and playfully pawed at Dana, trying to get a piece for himself.

"Oh, Wally," Dana laughed, "always the opportunist."

Wally then moved to work on Benny.

"The only time your cat is nice to me is if I have food on my plate," Benny said, smiling.

They continued to eat, cherishing every bite, every moment. After a while, Dana leaned back in her lounge chair, taking in the sprawling view of the Pacific, the jungle, and the ever-changing colors of the sky.

Unlike the faint constellations she used to squint to see in San Francisco, the heavens here sprawled in a tapestry of twinkling luminosity. The absence of city lights and pollution in this slice of Costa Rica allowed the sky to reveal its true splendor. It was as if she had traded the artificial glow of the city for the ethereal glow of the cosmos. Star clusters she hadn't known existed emerged from the darkness, and the Milky Way painted a broad, misty stroke across the expansive night canvas. Every glimmer felt closer, more personal, as if Mariposa Beach held a special ticket to the universe's grandest show.

"I never tire of looking up at the sky at night down here," Dana murmured, her voice filled with wonder.

Benny simply nodded.

"You know, Benny, every time I sit here, I'm reminded of how blessed I am. This... all of this"—she waved her hand to encompass the view, the house, and their shared life—"is like a dream."

He took her hand, intertwining his fingers with hers, and smiled. "It's not a dream, it's all real."

And in that moment, with the world bathed in twilight and the gentle sound of waves in the background, Dana truly felt at home. Her journey, with all its trials and tribulations, had led her to this perfect moment in Mariposa Beach.

AUTHOR NOTE

Hi there, and a heartfelt thank you for diving into my book! Your role as a reader is invaluable — it's you who truly brings these stories to life.

I'd be incredibly grateful if you could spare a moment to share your thoughts and rate this book on Amazon. Your feedback is not just appreciated; it's a guiding light for fellow readers navigating through the sea of books on Amazon.

Thank You!

ABOUT THE AUTHOR

I was born and raised in Costa Rica, but now live in San Francisco, California. I've always loved cozy mysteries, so when I decided to write one, I just knew I had to base it my home country. Although Mariposa Beach is a made up beach town, it's based on the lovely little communities that dot the Guanacaste Province.

You can learn more about me and my books over at my website: www.KCAmes.com.

Sign up for my newsletter for book updates, animal pics, and my recipe book of traditional Costa Rica dishes, for free:

kcames.com/subscribe

Find me online and say hello...

ALSO BY K.C. AMES

Mariposa Beach Cozy Mystery Books

Book 1: A Beach House to Die For

Book 2: A Book to Die For

Book 3: A Reality Show to Die For

Book 4: An Orchid to Die For

Book 5: A Podcast to Die For

Book 6: A Christmas to Die For

Book 7: A Parrot to Die For

Visit www.KCAmes.com for more information on these books.